NINA SONI
MASTER OF THE GARDEN

Written by **Kashmira Sheth**
Illustrated by **Jenn Kocsmiersky**

PEACHTREE
ATLANTA

Here is a list of things
people have said about Nina Soni.

"Nina Soni is many things: Indian American, a list-maker, a word-definer, and a big sister. She is funny, observant, and smart, and she can also sometimes be a bit forgetful. The number one thing that Nina is? Loveable! I adore Nina and know readers will, too."

—Debbi Michiko Florence, author of
the *Jasmine Toguchi* series

"A perfect fit for readers who enjoy realistic fiction about friendship and self-discovery."

—*School Library Journal*

"...a flawed but refreshing and very likable protagonist..."
—*Booklist*

"A sweet and entertaining series opener about family and friendship."

—*Kirkus Reviews*

She's a phenomenon!

Phe-no-me-non means a happening or an event.

In loving memory of my grandparents,
Champaklal and Kapilaben Trivedi, and the
tropical, magical garden of my childhood

–K. S.

Ω

Published by
PEACHTREE PUBLISHING COMPANY INC.
1700 Chattahoochee Avenue
Atlanta, Georgia 30318-2112
www.peachtree-online.com

Text © 2021 by Kashmira Sheth
Illustrations © 2021 by Jenn Kocsmiersky

Edited by Kathy Landwehr
Design and composition by Adela Pons

The illustrations were rendered digitally.

Printed in January 2021 in the United States of America by Lake Book Manufacturing in
Melrose Park, Illinois
10 9 8 7 6 5 4 3 2 1 (hardcover)
10 9 8 7 6 5 4 3 2 1 (trade paperback)
First Edition
HC ISBN 978-1-68263-225-3
PB ISBN 978-1-68263-226-0

Cataloging-in-Publication Data is available from the Library of Congress.

CHAPTER ONE

My luck had finally arrived!

I opened my bedroom window a crack and sniffed. Yes, it was here. I could tell just by the scent of the air. It had a warm, rich, earthy smell to it. The sun was shining, the forget-me-not-blue flower sky was clear and there was not a speck of snow anywhere.

Almost every year in Wisconsin, Take Our Daughters and Sons to Work Day is cold, snowy, rainy, windy, or a combination. That meant I usually ended up inside, doing computer work with Dad or helping Mom order seeds or plan a garden for someone. Dad loves his software engineering work but it is difficult to understand and I can't do much to help. Ordering seeds is about as exciting as watching my sister Kavita sing—not very enjoyable. And it is no fun to plan a garden but not plant it.

This year the weather was beautiful and I couldn't wait to start digging. Mom is a landscape architect, so today Kavita and I could garden with her.

Kavita is in first grade, so she was more into playing than planting. I am in fourth grade so this was going to be my responsibility.

Re-spon-si-bil-i-ty means something rests on your shoulders and you must take care of it.

I came downstairs to the kitchen. Luckily, Mom was already there.

"Mom, isn't it a nice day to garden?" I asked.

"Sure is," Kavita said.

She must have followed me quietly.

Mom looked out the window. "Yes, plenty of sunshine and no wind."

I had a bowl of oatmeal and Kavita had Cheerios. We topped our breakfasts with banana slices and blueberries. They were both easy to prepare, eat, and clean up afterward. On a busy and important day, it is smart to make a super-fast breakfast choice. It saves time and energy.

As she took her empty bowl to the sink, Kavita sang the same song over and over again. *"Garden, garden, dig and plant. Garden, garden, water and weed. Garden, garden, harvest and feast."*

OK, I was also excited about the garden. But I was not ready to listen to Kavita singing about it a thousand times over.

I loaded the bowls into the dishwasher. "Why don't you save your energy for digging?"

"Only people with little energy worry about saving it." She spread her arms wide. "I have a lot of energy so I can use it as much as I want."

"Still, shouldn't you be careful? It's like saving money. You don't want to spend it just because you have it."

Kavita was quiet. That meant she was thinking. She has always loved to sing. I have always tried to discourage her, especially in public. But it hasn't worked. Kavita has her own mind. Though it took me a long time to understand that, I still forget sometimes.

I kind of like that Kavita is her own person. Most of the time, I mean. I also have my own mind, but it's not a singing mind. It's a list-making mind.

Here is the in-my-head list of why a list-making mind is so useful.

* It keeps me organized.

* It keeps me focused.

* It keeps me kind of interesting. (It's not that I am boring but sometimes I think Kavita's singing is slightly more attention-grabbing).

Attention-grabbing or not, it was time to get going on Take Our Daughters and Sons to Work Day.

"Are you ready, Mom?" I asked.

"I want to have my chai first."

In my excitement I had forgotten that Mom and Dad need their tea before they start their mornings. Until they drink their chai, they are as slow as slugs.

Only after they chug their chai, which is really tea with ginger, spices, and milk, do they become nonsluggish. Then they start darting like rabbits from here to there.

Kavita took out paper and crayons from her art box. She spread them on the dining table. As she colored she sang again. *"Garden, garden, dig and plant."*

I shook my head.

She saw me and stopped. "Nina, I sing because I don't want to burst."

"You can't burst." I walked closer to her. "Have you ever seen anyone burst?"

"A balloon."

"You're not filled with air."

She smoothed out the paper with her hands. "When I sleep I gather a lot of energy and when I am awake I use it, right?"

"Sounds right to me." I looked at Kavita's drawing, a diagram of a garden. It was filled with plants of different heights and colors. Impressive!

Im-pres-sive means something that makes you go "Wow!"

She had drawn vines with peapods hanging on them, plants full of red and green peppers, and a row of something else, but I couldn't tell what it was. Maybe it was some kind of a root crop.

Kavita shook my arm. "Why aren't you answering me?"

I looked at her. "What's your question?"

She rested her hands on the table. "OK. I will repeat it one more time. But that's it."

"Try me."

"If I don't use up any energy, then I will have too much of it. And if all that energy doesn't burst me, wouldn't it hurt?"

"Why would it hurt?"

"If you eat too much, you overstuff your stomach. It doesn't burst your tummy, but it hurts. If you overstuff your body with energy, it will hurt."

"Today we're going to garden and you'll spend energy." I made a circle with my arm to show how much. "A lot of it."

She picked up another crayon and began coloring furiously. I guess she wasn't spending any energy listening to me.

"How long have you been working on your drawing?" I asked.

"For a week." She picked up the paper and showed it to me. "Do you like it?"

It looked even better when she held it up. "I do."

"Mom says it is good to make plans before you plant."

I nodded.

"So, this is my plan. I know exactly what I am going to plant. Where I am going to plant. And how the plants will look."

I, a fourth grader, a list maker, was the one who had asked Mom if we could have our own vegetable plots.

But my sister, a first grader, a singer, had already drawn her garden plan.

Why hadn't I?

Now I was, kind of, not happy with myself.

I glanced at Mom and Dad. They were just getting ready to drink their chai. I had time.

I went back to my room and opened Sakhi.

Sakhi means friend in Hindi.

I have named my notebook. It is good to name a notebook that is special to you. Because then you feel like you can tell your notebook all your secrets. I write just about everything in Sakhi—mostly lists. Sakhi is a good friend and is always ready for me to tell her new things.

My garden list

* Draw a diagram of a garden.

* Fill the patch with good soil and compost.

* Make a list of vegetables to plant.

* Get seeds (Mom probably already has seeds) and plant them.
* Water (only if it doesn't rain) and weed.
* Harvest and eat.

The last two on the list sounded a lot like Kavita's song.

That was OK, I told myself. Sometimes Kavita's songs do make sense. This was one of them.

Then I had another idea. What if we have too many vegetables? What could we do with them?

I opened a new page in Sakhi and started writing.

Business plan to sell extra vegetables

* Advertise by making up flyers for neighbors.
* Mention location, time, and vegetables that are available.
* Arrange vegetables in baskets.
* Make signs with prices.

✳ Give free samples.

✳ Hand out recipes.

This was perfect!

I rushed back downstairs.

"Mom, can I use your pencils to draw my garden plan?" Mom has several fancy mechanical pencils and colored pencils. She uses them when she draws shrubs, walkways, trees, and flowers on her plans, which show her clients what their gardens will look like.

"Please use the ones that are on the table. Don't open any new packs or boxes. As soon as I finish my chai and change, will start our project."

"Thanks," I said.

I held one of Mom's pencils and doodled—but not with the pencil and not on a piece of paper. It was as if each thought I had was a pencil and my mind was a blank piece of paper. I doodled in my head—imaginary plants with imaginary vegetables growing on them.

Without thinking, I switched to list making.

Here is my in-my-head list

* April is almost over.

* That means I can start planting soon.

* It will be fun to take care of the plants and watch them grow, grow, grow.

* Butterflies will visit and hummingbirds will flap their wings like crazy.

* The bees will find nectar and the earthworms will find a home.

* By the end of summer, I will have a beautiful garden with tons of vegetables.

* We will be able to eat and sell fresh, crunchy vegetables.

* With luck, I will be master of the garden.

Nina Soni, Master of the Garden!

It had a healthy, nutritious sound to it.

I kept munching on the idea, over and over again.

CHAPTER TWO

The doorbell rang. Since Dad was nowhere in sight and Mom was getting ready, I looked through the glass panel to see who it was.

Jay, my best friend, gave me a thumbs-up sign through the window. What was he doing here? I put the pencil down, stopped the in-my-head plan making, and opened the door.

"Hi, Nina!" Jay said.

"Jay! Yay!" Kavita yelled from the dining room. She sure knows his voice.

Before I could ask Jay why he had come, he said, "Looks like you're ready to garden."

"How do you know?"

"Because your mom invited me to garden. Also, you're wearing old pants that are too short on you."

I rolled my eyes as I went to the kitchen. How come Jay always notices things about me when I don't want him to? How come Mom didn't tell me she'd invited Jay?

He followed. "Did you have breakfast?"

"Yes. Are you hungry?"

"Only if you have something yummy." Jay loves the fresh Indian breads Mom makes. But we didn't have any leftovers from last night.

"Sorry, no paratha or roti. I had oatmeal," I said.

"No, thanks. Not hungry."

Mom walked in. "Jay, right on time. Ready?"

He took off his jacket and hung it on one of the counter stools.

I stared. Jay was wearing a T-shirt with a picture of a

pile of dirt and a shovel and the words *Let's Dig* in large letters.

Sure, Jay is my best friend, but he wears some really strange T-shirts. He has one that says *Ask Me How to Dance.* Now this one had a picture of a shovel. At least it didn't say *Ask Me How to Garden.*

"Aren't you going with your mom or dad to their work?" I asked.

"Nope. I'm here to garden."

"Yay!" Kavita said.

I was happy too. I mean gardening with Kavita was fun. But gardening with Kavita and Jay was going to be double the fun!

The trouble with my brain is that when something new comes in, the old plan kind of gets derailed.

De-railed means that something doesn't stay on its track.

Drawing my garden went off when I started brain-doodling. Then Jay came in. Now even brain-doodling was off my thinking track.

And really it was for the best because Mom was ready.

I pointed at the door. "Let's go out."

"Not yet," Mom said. She sat at the dining table. We gathered around her. "So, what is the first thing we should consider when we have a garden?" she asked.

Oh no, she was turning this into a lesson. Jay and I glanced at each other.

Kavita raised her hand. I guess she also thought this was a class.

"Yes, Kavita," Mom said.

"Follow my plan."

"We'll do that." Mom smiled. "What are the things plants need to grow?"

"Songs, seeds, and shovels!" Kavita shouted.

"You supply songs," Mom said to Kavita. Then she gestured toward Jay and me. "Nina and Jay will supply shovels and I will supply seeds."

Jay and I needed to step up. I raised my hand. Jay elbowed me. I ignored him.

"Nina," Mom said.

"Sun, soil, and water." There! I had listed the rest of the thing plants need.

"I have chosen the spot that gets the most sun," Mom said.

"But I thought we were going to grow our vegetables in the same plot you do," I said.

Mom's eyes twinkled. "We're going to make new garden beds by the left side of the garage. Raised garden beds."

"What about the lawn growing there?" Jay asked.

"We must put down something so that the grass doesn't grow. What would be good material to use for that?"

"Feet," Kavita said. "We can run on the grass and trample it."

"I don't think feet is the material Mom is thinking of," I said.

Kavita looked at Mom. "Feet is the best material, right?

Mrs. Crump said, 'Don't trample my grass. You'll kill it.'"

"Kavita, Mrs. Crump said that after she had planted a new lawn. She didn't want you to walk on it. This grass has been there for a long time. It'll be harder to get rid of. We have to use something else to remove it," Mom said. "I have a pile of newspaper in the garage. Can you three bring it out while I get the kiddie swimming pool?"

Mom was making no sense, but we followed her to the garage. She took down the plastic mermaid pool Kavita used last summer. There were spiderwebs on it. Mom didn't seem to mind them. I guess if you work in the garden, you kind of have to get used to bugs and bees.

Kavita, Jay, and I grabbed newspapers. Mom filled the pool with water. "Please soak the newspapers in here," she told us.

Kavita dunked the newspapers she was carrying. "Gardening is so much fun!"

"We haven't started yet," I said.

"Aren't you here to garden, Jay?" Kavita asked him.

"Yes," he replied.

She turned to me. "And that's what we're doing."

Sometimes it is easier to agree with Kavita than to argue with her. It saves me energy.

"OK," I said. "What next, Mom?"

"The newspapers need to soak for a while. Let's go into the dining room."

Inside, Mom picked up a roll of paper that was on the windowsill. Mom has a lot of plans around our house, so I am used to seeing rolls of paper on the windowsills, the dining table, or the kitchen counter. I usually don't pay much attention to them. But this one was for *our* garden.

Mom spread the roll out on the table. The plan showed three side-by-side rectangular garden beds. They were the same shape as Kavita's, but they didn't look the same. Instead of drawings of plants, the rectangles had measurements written on them.

Height 2ft., length 3ft., width 2 ft.

21

2 ft.		2 ft.		2 ft.	
3 ft.		3 ft.		3 ft.	

"Did you know anything about this?" I asked Jay.

"No."

Of course, he didn't know. How could he have? My mom had drawn it, not his.

"I knew about it," Kavita said. "I saw Mom working on it last week, then I listened to her and Meera Masi talk about the garden, then I heard her ask Dad if he could help."

"You're an excellent spy, Kavita," Jay said.

"I am?"

"Better than Nina. She didn't notice any of this."

I wasn't going to let Jay get away with that. "Well, you didn't notice your mom talking to my mom, did you?"

Kavita slid her paper in front of us. "Now listen," she said. "This is how we're going to plant. Peas in the middle, peppers on the side, potatoes on top and bottom."

I waited for more. No more words came out of her mouth. Kavita's garden project was too easy. I didn't say anything. The less I say to her, the more energy I have to concentrate on being a master of the garden. That way I would have tons of vegetables.

Con-cen-trate means to really make something a center and pay attention to it.

Roar! I could hear the lawn mower!

It was Dad. I mean Dad wasn't the lawn mower, Dad was mowing the lawn. Every time he passed the dining room window, we had to talk louder in order to hear each other.

"There will be three raised beds," I said. "Does that mean one for Jay, one for Kavita, and one for me?"

"I suppose," Mom said.

"Great. Then we don't all have to plant only vegetables that start with *P*." I was relieved.

Re-lieved means to feel like you can let go of the breath you're holding in.

Mom slipped each of us a piece of paper. "Here is a list of vegetables. Pick out a few you want to plant."

"Maybe I can also plant pomegranates. They start with *P*." Kavita clapped. "And I love them."

Then she proved how much she loved them by singing, "*Juicy, juicy, oh-so-fruity. Pomegranate, pretty and pouchy.*"

"How can a pomegranate be pouchy?" I asked.

"Like a pouch, a pomegranate holds yummy red seeds. And all those seeds are tiny pouches filled with juice," she said.

Jay's eyes widened. "That makes sense!"

I couldn't argue with that. It was true.

"Kavita, we can't grow pomegranates in Wisconsin. It's too cold here," Mom explained.

"Then I will just grow peas, peppers, and potatoes," Kavita said.

I studied the diagram again.

Three raised beds.

2 ft.		2 ft.		2 ft.	
3 ft.	☐	3 ft.	☐	3 ft.	☐

"This will take a long time to build," I said. "Will someone help us?"

"Yes," Mom said, pointing out the window. I turned around. Jay's parents were helping Dad drag things out of the garage.

"What are Meera Masi and Uncle Ryan doing outside?" I asked.

"Since my dad is in the construction business, he's going to help us," Jay said.

Mom rolled up the paper and we all went outside.

She spread the plans on our brand-new picnic bench. We all pored over them, even Dad, Meera Masi, and Uncle Ryan.

Usually Mom has two sets of plans, in case one gets lost or we spill something on it. Then she still has a clean copy to give her client. Today there was only one copy. I guess Mom was the planner and the client so we were taking our chances.

I heard a rumble.

A truck drove up. We all watched as it dumped compost in one corner of our driveway.

"That compost looks almost like the soil," Kavita said. "Why do we need it?"

"The compost is made from recycled vegetables, leaves, and manure that have been sitting in a pile for a long time," I explained. "It's super-good for the plants."

"Yay! That means our plants will grow super-well," Kavita said.

That did it.

I could almost feel my garden sprouting.

Another idea sprouted in my brain. How much money would we need to grow these vegetables?

My in-my-head list

* Mom and Dad had already paid for the wood and soil.

* We would need some seeds or plants, which usually cost money. Luckily, Mom already has

a lot of them and she had agreed to share.

* And after that everything else would be free—rain, sunshine, air, space, earthworms.

* And our labor.

* We could certainly harvest a lot more vegetables than we could eat.

* We could sell, sell, sell the rest.

* That means our business would take off and we could make a lot of money.

My palms itched for all the vegetables I was going to harvest and sell. I already had a business plan. I didn't have the name for my business, but I didn't need it right away. That is because even spinach and lettuce take many weeks to grow. And they are some of the earliest plants I have seen at the farmers' market.

"What are you thinking?" Jay smiled. "Cooking up some special project?"

I gestured with my hand. "Why not?"

"What is it?"

"Let's start," Dad called.

"Later," I said to Jay.

I wasn't ready to share my selling plan with Jay yet.

CHAPTER THREE

And then the fun began.

Jay and I helped Dad lug cedar wood pieces from the back of our van trunk. Uncle Ryan cut the boards in three-foot and two-foot pieces.

Kavita sang, *"Cedar wood, cedar wood, you sure smell spiffy! Cedar wood, cedar wood, help grow our garden in a jiffy."*

"The wood is not going to help the garden grow," Jay said.

"He is right," I said. "Mom, do we need raised beds? Couldn't we grow the plants where the grass was growing?"

"Our clay soil is not conducive for a garden," Mom replied.

"What does that mean?" Kavita asked

"Conducive means it is not very good to grow the plants in," I said.

Kavita beamed. "Then I was right. Without the wood, we won't have raised bed. No bed, no good soil. And no garden."

"She is right," Dad said.

"I always am," Kavita said.

My sister thinks she is always right. It is best to stay quiet about it.

"The boards are two inches wide and eight inches tall. If we want our beds two feet tall, how many do we need to stack up?" Mom asked.

Mom really had turned this into a classroom.

I did mental math.

One foot is 12 inches.

8 inches in each board x 3 boards = 24 inches.

That means we needed three boards to make our beds two feet high.

Before I could answer, Kavita said, "Three boards."

"How did you do the math so fast?" I asked.

"I counted the boards Mom has on the drawings. There are three of them, see?"

"Not only is she a great spy, she is a great mathematician," Jay said.

"And don't forget, I am also a great singer and song maker," Kavita added.

"My sister, the most humble person ever."

Kavita looked confused. "What does that mean?"

"Nina is being sarcastic," Jay said.

"What does that mean?"

"Sarcastic means I really didn't mean what I said," I told her.

Kavita looked double confused. "What didn't you mean?"

"That you're humble," Jay said.

"It's OK." She waved her hand. "I don't even know what humble means. And I don't want to know."

"Stop talking and come help," Mom called.

The freshly mowed grass was short and Mom sprinkled a white powder to outline a large rectangle on it. "This is lime, which is powdered calcium carbonate," she said. "It can affect the soil's chemistry—turning it from sour to sweet, which is good for some kinds of plants. It is also very handy to use to outline an area. Please cover the space inside the lines with a thick layer of wet newspapers."

Jay, Kavita, and I brought the soaked newspapers and covered the area completely.

"Perfect," Mom said. "This will kill the grass and stop the weeds from growing."

"Now it's time to build the raised beds," Uncle Ryan said.

Jay and I ran to him.

"We're ready," I said.

I watched while Uncle Ryan held two boards in place and Jay nailed them together.

"Can I try?" I asked.

Jay handed me a nail. Then a hammer.

"I have never nailed before," I said.

"First time for everything," Jay said.

I was surprised he didn't make fun of me for not knowing how to nail.

"Be careful. Watch where you hit," Uncle Ryan warned.

I started. The first pound was good. The second landed on my fingers. "Ouch!"

I did three more pounds before I hit my fingers again.

"After the nail goes in a little, you don't have to hold it. It will keep going in as you pound," Jay said.

"Thanks. You should have told me earlier."

"You should have been more careful," Jay said, hammering in his own nail. "Ouch!"

Uncle Ryan shook his head. "Follow your own advice, Jay."

"Yes, Dad."

I gave Jay a look that meant *Yeah! Follow your own advice, Jay!*

Once the wooden frames were made, Uncle Ryan built a ledge around the top of each one. That way we'd have a place to sit when we worked on our gardens. When he was done, we piled the soil and compost mix in them. That went pretty fast.

By the time we were done building and filling the beds, we were starving. No one had thought about making lunch, and everyone was tired. The fastest meal to fix and eat was bread and fresh cheese curds along with carrot sticks and bell pepper slices. Kavita, Jay, and I washed our hands and took the food outside.

"I think the cheese curd I just had was the freshest," I said, after I finished chewing one.

"How do you know?" Kavita asked.

"Because it squeaked the loudest."

"It's because you are chewing yours and they sound loudest to you. Mine sound loudest to me," Jay said.

The sun went behind the clouds and it felt a little chilly. I rubbed my palms. "I guess."

Kavita raised her hand. I guess she was still acting like we were in a classroom.

I pointed at her. "Yes, Kavita?"

"My cheese curds are the freshest."

"Why?"

"Because I am the youngest, so my teeth are freshest. And when cheese curds touch them, they become fresher."

Jay glanced at me and sighed. "You're right, Kavita."

I stuffed my mouth with more cheese curds.

Now I had peace in my head, squeaks in my ears, and good taste in my mouth.

∗∗∗

After lunch, everyone was tired. Meera Masi and Uncle Ryan went home, but Jay hung around. I was glad. Lately Jay had been busy with his cousins and hadn't spent as much time at our house as he used to. Kavita's friend Avery also came over for the afternoon. That meant that Jay and I had time to do our own things without having to pay attention to Kavita.

I thought about telling Jay about my fabulous veggie-selling idea. We could work on it together. Would he think it was silly? I mean, nothing was planted and nothing was growing. Maybe I needed to plan a little more before talking to Jay about the business.

The important part now was to prepare for planting. Without planting, there won't be any harvest or selling.

"Jay, lets plan out our gardens," I said.

"What's there to plan? Just drop the seeds in the soil and watch them grow."

"Didn't you see how nice Kavita's plan looks?"

"The paper garden?" he snorted. "Sure. But that doesn't mean her actual garden will look that nice."

"Why not?"

He shrugged. "Gardens always look nice in drawings or photos. Wait, I'll show you."

Jay picked up one of the catalogs from the table and flipped through the pages. "See, these flowers are gorgeous. Not like real ones."

I pointed to the daffodils and hyacinths outside. "My mom's garden is beautiful."

"Your mom is an expert. Have you ever seen my mom's garden look that nice?"

Jay was right. Meera Masi's garden is usually a mess. Sometimes Mom helps her clean up and replant. I didn't want to be rude, so I didn't say that. "But your mom is an amazing dancer. My mom can't do that."

"I guess so." Jay shrugged. "Though I have never seen your mom dance."

"That's the proof, she can't. So, what should we do now?"

Jay's green eyes, the color of spring shoots, sparkled. "Let's make a plan to convince Ms. Lapin to give us gardening credit."

To con-vince means to make someone agree to do what you want them to do.

"Like as a science project?" I asked. Ms. Lapin is our teacher.

"Yup."

I was excited about that. I had gotten a B+ on my last science quiz. If Jay and I could convince Ms. Lapin to give us extra credit, I was all for it.

We went to my room. I took out Sakhi and Jay and I made a list.

Gardening extra credit plan

* We could ask Ms. Lapin for a garden plot at school.

* But then we would have to work twice as hard, keeping a garden at home and a garden at school.

* Also, who would take care of the garden at school during summer vacation?

* We needed to get credit for our home garden.

* We could share pictures of our home garden at school. In the summer, we could keep a journal about our plants.

* Yes, a teacher always likes to know what we do during the summer break.

✳ We could include what we learned from our experiences and our gardening experiments.

That was it. We should ask Ms. Lapin for extra credit. That way my B+ in science could easily become an A or even an A+!

I wondered if Jay also needed extra credit to pull up his grade. Maybe that's why he suggested this idea. I didn't ask him though.

Sometimes friendship is like that. You kind of know the answer before you ask. And Jay probably knew that I could also use extra credit.

He smiled at me. "I think this plan should work."

I closed Sakhi. "That way we can have two rewards: crunchy, crisp veggies and extra-crunchy, extra-crisp credits."

"Like just-plucked peas," Jay said.

Then something occurred to me.

Jay must have seen it on my face. "What's the problem?" he asked.

"I don't think we should ask Ms. Lapin for credit for our gardens at home."

"Why not?"

"Because not everyone has a yard or space to garden. It wouldn't be fair to them if they can't get extra credit."

He was quiet.

"Jay?"

He looked at me. "They might feel bad about saying that in front of everyone in the class."

"I would. Do you remember our apartment before we moved to our house?"

Jay nodded.

"We couldn't have had a garden there even if we wanted to."

"We won't ask for extra credit." Then he smiled. "Nina, wasn't it a good idea though?"

"It certainly was. Now I have to work hard in science to bring up my grade on the next quiz."

Jay laughed. "Me too."

CHAPTER FOUR

Jay and I went downstairs, "Can we plant seeds now?" I asked Mom.

She glanced out the window. "The wind has picked up and it's cloudy now. Maybe we should wait until the weekend to plant the seeds."

Jay looked disappointed. "I won't be able to come this weekend."

It wouldn't be fun gardening without him. "Can Jay come after school tomorrow? Could we do it then?"

Mom looked up the weather on her phone. "Yes, it will be little chilly, but sunny."

"I will bring my warm jacket, just in case," Jay said.

"Wear a jacket, plant a garden. Wear mittens and dig deep. When you're finished, have some hot cocoa," Kavita sang.

"It will be clear, so you won't need mittens tomorrow afternoon, Kavita," Mom said.

"Did Avery leave?" I asked.

"Yes," Kavita replied.

"We have a bag of sweet potatoes at home," Jay said. "A couple of them have sprouted. Can I plant them? Will they grow?"

Was he making this up? "Is it your job to inspect sweet potatoes in your house?" I asked.

"Ha ha! Very funny, Nina," Jay said. "My mom was planning to cook them last night and noticed they were old. She was going to throw them out so I asked if I could do an experiment with them."

"Gardening is not an experiment," Kavita said.

"It can be," Jay said. He turned to Mom. "Can't it?"

"It sure can," Mom replied. "You can use those sweet potatoes, but you must wait to plant them until the soil warms up."

"Like next week?"

"Like a month from now," Mom said.

"In a month the sweet potatoes will be really old and stinky," Jay said.

"Yup," I agreed. "Maybe you should plant something else."

The phone rang.

"Hi," Mom answered. She listened for a while before saying, "I'm sure Nina will be thrilled, but let me ask her." Then she turned to me. "Megan's mom is on the phone. They have had something come up. She is wondering if Megan can come over this evening. It is fine with me."

"Yes," I said. We had planned to plant the garden today. Then we couldn't do that and I was sad. So, my friend Megan coming over was a good surprise.

"Yes, that should work," Mom said and then handed me the phone. "Megan wants to talk to you."

"Hi Megan."

"Nina, I have some homework, but I'll finish it now. Can we cook tonight? Is Kavita at home? I was—"

"Let me ask my mom about cooking," I said. Megan loves to talk on the phone. It is as if the phone supplies her words that she can just spill out. She would have kept talking and talking, so I had to interrupt. Mom nodded at me. "My mom says we can cook and Kavita is home."

"I can't wait to see you!" Megan said.

Only after we had hung up I wondered why Megan wanted to know if Kavita was home.

Jay asked, "So what are you cooking tonight?"

I shrugged. I hadn't thought about that. "Megan likes homemade pizzas. Could we have pizza tonight, Mom?"

"Sure." Mom turned to Jay. "I'll call your Mom."

He beamed. Mom knows Jay loves her pizza.

"Yay, yay!" Kavita said. "We will do a singing show. That's what Megan told me we can do next time we're together. I'm sure she will bring her ukually."

"It is *ukulele*," I said.

45

"Ukually," Kavita repeated. "Jay, do you know how to play one?"

"No."

"I can teach you," Kavita said.

"You don't know how," I said.

Kavita put her hands on her hips. "I do. OK?"

Sometime little sisters can be bossy and unreasonable. But I was going to cook with Jay and Megan. We were going to make pizzas. I was happy. When you are happy nothing bothers you. So today, it was easy to ignore Kavita.

✳✳✳

Kavita had been right. Megan arrived carrying her ukulele. They were planning to play and sing. That's why Megan had asked if Kavita was home.

First we made pizzas though. Mom had already prepared the dough. She removed the tea towel that had covered it while it rose.

Kavita got on her tiptoes and peeked at it. "Has it doubled in size, Mom?"

"Yes. Wash your hands before you touch it," Mom said.

Kavita washed and dried her hands. Jay, Megan, and I did too.

"The best part about making pizza is beating up the dough," Kavita said as she put her fists through it.

"It's not beating up. It's punching down," I said.

"Beating or punching, it's all the same."

"When you're done beating," Jay said, "give it to me and I will roll it out."

I looked at Jay. Sometimes he has more patience with Kavita than I do. And today he knew that, because he smiled at me.

Megan and Jay rolled out the dough. I like to do that but today I let them. We make Indian bread most every day and I often get to roll the dough.

We made cheese pizzas for ourselves and spicy-banana-pepper-and-garlic pizza for Mom and Dad. They like very spicy food! Way too much.

After we ate, it was time for our show. First Kavita and I did an Indian dance that we had learned from Jay's mom.

It was with flowy hand and body movements and some pirouettes.

Then Megan did some tap dancing without tap shoes.

"Should we play ukually and sing now?" Kavita asked.

Jay stood up. "What about my turn?"

"You want to dance?" I asked.

"Of course," he said. Then he started.

My mouth fell open. Jay was break dancing! One minute he was upright and the next, he was on the ground.

He twisted his legs and arms like they were spaghetti. I had never seen him do it before.

"When did you learn to do that?" I asked.

"Remember the T-shirt I have?"

"The one that says *Ask Me How to Dance*?" I said. "You only got that a little while ago. Is that when you started taking classes?"

"A little before that."

"And you kept it a secret?" I asked.

"I wanted to surprise you."

"You certainly did!"

We were all so impressed with Jay that we asked him to dance again.

Then it was time for Megan and Jay to go home. Kavita complained. "I never got a chance to play the ukually."

"I'm going to start guitar lessons," Megan said. "Kavita, if you want my ukulele, it's yours."

Megan was giving it away to Kavita. Wow! I was a tiny bit jealous.

Kavita was so shocked that she lost her tongue. "What do you say, Kavita?" Mom reminded her.

Silence.

"Kavita?"

Kavita ran over and gave Megan a hug. "You are the best. Thank you!"

That night Kavita played ukulele in her bedroom. It was so screechy and scratchy that I had to hide in my room, close the door, and get under my blanket. She wanted to sleep with it too. Mom and Dad said she couldn't, so Kavita placed the ukulele on her nightstand.

I hoped she wouldn't get up in the middle of the night to play it.

When I closed my eyes, I could still see Jay's amazing dancing. Maybe he could entertain while we sold our vegetables. He would attract a lot of people and that would mean good foot traffic. I mean it wouldn't be a lot of cars and buses but maybe a lot of would-be customer traffic. And that could turn in to good buying-traffic.

Then I had the scariest thought. What if Kavita also wanted to play her ukulele? Not just people would run away—so would potatoes and peas.

CHAPTER FIVE

On Friday, Jay, Kavita, and I walked to school together. Kavita went to her first-grade class, while Jay and I went to our fourth-grade one. Jay took off his hoodie and hung it in his cubby.

He was wearing the same T-shirt with a drawing of a shovel and a pile of dirt that he had worn yesterday.

"Hi Nina," Tyler said. "Jay said you did a garden project together for the Take Our Daughters and Sons to Work Day."

"Yes. It was great. What did you do?" I asked as we walked into the classroom.

"I went to work with my dad. He gave this seminar on something financial something. Boring!"

I laughed, then scooted my chair closer to my desk and leaned over. "Jay, are you wearing a dirty T-shirt today?"

"No. I washed it last night."

"Then how come the pile of dirt is still there?"

He didn't crack a smile. "Ha, ha! Very funny."

"Hey, do you want some seeds for your garden?"

"What?" Jay looked confused.

"Should I glue some tomato seeds right onto your T-shirt to see if they sprout?"

We both giggled.

"Care to share your funny story, Nina? Jay?" Ms. Lapin asked.

I hadn't heard the second bell ring. But it must have. How could I share my silly thought with Ms. Lapin? So I stayed quiet. Jay did too. She didn't pursue it.

> To pur-sue means to follow something until you catch it.

I was glad Ms. Lapin didn't want to catch our giggles.

After that I tried to pay attention. Ms. Lapin had already noticed us laughing once. It would be disrespectful to do that again.

> **Dis-re-spect-ful** means when you behave like you don't care for other people's feelings.

"Would anyone like to share what they did for Take our Daughters and Sons to Work Day?" Ms. Lapin asked.

Tyler groaned. A few of us raised our hands.

"Kyle?" Ms. Lapin said.

"I went with my mom to the gym and attended her Zumba class," Kyle said.

"That sounds like a fun way to exercise," Ms. Lapin looked around. "Jay?"

"Nina, her sister Kavita, and I helped our parents built three raised garden beds. We will be planting seeds today."

"Do you know what you'll be growing, Jay, Nina?"

Jay glanced at me. "We haven't decided yet."

"Kavita is planting peas, potatoes, and peppers," I said and almost tripped up on all the words starting with the letter P.

Ms. Lapin smiled. "Anyone else want to share?"

"I helped my parents in our cheese and wine shop. I wasn't allowed to touch the wine bottles though," Emma said.

Everyone laughed.

Then Ms. Lapin asked us to work on our math problems.

All through the morning a tiny part of me wanted to ask for extra credit for gardening, even though I knew it was not a good thing to do. Sometimes my mind wants to do things that I know are not right or good.

The picture that Kavita had drawn of her garden kept popping up in my head. Then I added a few more details in my imagination, like fluttering butterflies, wiggling earthworms, and hanging beans.

Today I wanted to do what was right. So I shooed away the butterflies, sent the earthworms under the soil, ignored the beans, and kept my mouth shut.

Later, during science Ms. Lapin told us, "You will have one more quiz before the finals."

"We can work hard to get As. Right?" Jay whispered to me.

I didn't want Ms. Lapin to get upset at us again, so I just smiled and nodded.

It was difficult to stay quiet about the extra credit, not think about the garden, not answer Jay, but it was the respectful thing to do.

✳✳✳

After school, Jay, Kavita, and I rushed home. Mom took out seed packets as soon as we walked in the house.

"Decide what you want to plant in your garden plot," she said. "Pick out one type of vegetable that will mature early, one that will be ready mid-season, and one that will be available later. That will create a good balance."

"What does that mean?" Kavita asked.

"Something like peas or spinach needs cool weather; that's when they grow best. They will be ready to eat in

56

late spring. Plants like tomatoes and peppers need warm weather and heat to grow. You plant them later and harvest them in late summer. Some crops like pumpkins need a long time to grow. You plant them early and harvest them in fall."

"What about potatoes, Mom?" Kavita asked.

"Good question," Mom replied. "There are early, middle, and late maturing varieties of potatoes, so it depends upon which you plant."

"I have an amazing idea. I'll plant a late variety of potatoes," Kavita said. "That way I'll have peas early, pepper in the middle, and potatoes in fall!

She really had chosen the right plants. I went through the seeds and picked out rainbow Swiss chard for my early crop and pole beans to harvest in summer. I couldn't decide on the third vegetable.

"Could I buy something to plant from a nursery or a farmers' market later?" I asked.

"Sure," Mom replied. "That's a good idea."

Jay took out spinach, tomato, and pumpkin seeds.

"Won't pumpkins need a lot of space to grow?" I asked.

"The package says these are bush variety. After I harvest my spinach, they can spread in that area," Jay said.

Mom nodded. "Now you all must read the instructions on the seed packages for all your vegetables to figure out when you can plant them and what they will need to grow."

"This says I need to start tomato plants in the house," Jay said.

"I'll give you small pots to start them inside," Mom said. "Make sure you water them just right."

Jay gave her a thumbs-up. "Spinach," he said, rattling the package. "It says early spring is the right planting time."

We all went outside. Mom asked, "Do you want to make rows or do square foot planting?"

Kavita clapped. "Is that like square dancing?"

"Sure. If you do square foot planting, you plant one crop in a one-by-one square foot. Your garden plot is two-feet by three-feet, so how many squares will you have?" Mom asked.

Again, a math lesson.

"Six," Jay answered.

Mom beamed.

I looked at him sideways. "Easy," I mouthed.

We each only had six squares. "I'm going to divide my plot in three parts and plant three crops in two squares each," I said.

"What if I get too many peas?" Kavita asked.

"We could sell the extra." I covered my mouth as soon as those words spilled out. I hadn't talked to my parents about my business. "Or we could barter," I added.

Kavita looked confused. "I don't know how to barter."

I explained. "To barter means you exchange one thing for another. If we barter, you can give me peas and I will give you Swiss chard. And you can give peas to Jay and get some of his spinach. No money needed."

"Now I know how to barter." Kavita twirled. "That will be fun!"

I made a shallow ditch where I would plant the Swiss

chard seeds. Just as I was about to drop them in, I read the instructions again. Oops!

"Mom, why do I have to soak these seeds for fifteen minutes?" I asked.

"It will help them germinate quicker."

"What does that word mean?" Kavita asked.

"Germinate means when the seed starts to grow into a plant," I said.

I went into the house, filled a cup with warm water, and put the seeds in to soak. Then I rushed back outside.

"What about pole beans," I asked. "Should I plant them now?"

"Read the label, please," Mom said.

Ugh! So I did.

"It says to wait until after the last frost date. Is it because they could die if there is a frost?" I asked.

"Yes. Our last frost date is May twentieth," Mom said.

"Then I will wait until May twentieth before I sow seeds."

"I can plant my peas now," Kavita said as she dropped the seeds in a furrow that Mom had helped her make.

"I've finished planting my spinach," Jay said.

I was the only one having no luck getting my seeds in the ground.

When you are at a party, fifteen minutes goes by quickly. But try soaking seeds for fifteen minutes! I did. It feels like it goes on forever. Even after I watched Kavita and Jay, made the furrows with a trowel, and reread the package instructions, it was still not time.

Then finally it was time to plant!

Swiss chard seeds are large so I was able to pick up one seed at a time. I dropped the seeds in the furrows I'd made, and then covered them with a layer of soil before watering the garden.

When we were done, we had some hot chocolate, and then it was time for Jay's dance class, so he left, taking the tomato seeds and a small tray of planters with him.

Back in my room, I made a list in Sakhi.

Why I love to garden

* I love digging in dirt, planting seeds, and watching things grow.

* I love the smell of earth, all earthwormy and crumbly.

* I love the butterflies, bees, and hummingbirds that visit the garden.

✳ I can't wait to harvest and eat crispy,
crunchy or juicy, plump vegetables.

I had planted my first seeds, in my first garden. For the next few months, I was going to give it all my attention. The beginning of things is very important. Your first word, your first step, getting your first tooth, losing your first tooth, your first bicycle, your first best friend—these are all things you remember. So you see, first is important.

I was going to do my best for my first garden. If it grew well, I would have enough vegetables to eat, barter, and sell. By planting a garden, I was making sure I had something to sell.

In a way, I had planted seeds of my first business. Ever.

✳✳✳

"Where are you going with that ukulele, Kavita?" I heard Mom say.

Kavita had her jacket and earmuffs on. But no mittens. I guess she couldn't play ukulele with mittened fingers.

"I'm going to sing to my plants."

"There are no plants yet. Only seeds," I said. *You also don't know how to play the ukulele yet*, I wanted to add.

Kavita slipped on her shoes. "The seeds might like to hear songs. And I'm sure the earthworms would too."

"It's cold and will get dark soon, Kavita," I said. "Your seeds are probably tired and need rest after the excitement of being put in the soil. You can sing to them tomorrow."

Kavita nodded. She placed her ukulele on a window seat and took off her jacket and earmuffs. Mom gave me a thumbs-up.

Then Kavita picked up the ukulele again. She began to play and sing. *"My garden, beautiful garden. Oh, my garden, amazing garden…"*

My ears were not happy with all that screechiness.

I don't know what else she sang because I went back upstairs, closed my door, and picked up a book.

When I am reading I usually don't pay attention to anything else. A story carries me into a different world.

I mean, my body stays in the same place, but my mind travels far away. Once I started reading, it distracted me from Kavita.

Dis-tract-ed means your mind forgets what you were doing because it gets busy with something else.

Now I had escaped my sister's music. Completely.

At least for the moment.

65

CHAPTER SiX

In the beginning I checked my garden often. When you first plant things, you have to wait, and wait, and wait for things to pop out of soil. Kavita's peas and Jay's spinach sprouted first. After about two weeks, my Swiss chard finally came in.

It was mid-May, almost a month since Take Our Daughters and Sons to Work Day. That Saturday, I couldn't wait to work in the garden. But first, I had to go to my dance class. It was only for an hour, so as soon as I got home, I took off my ankle bells and dance clothes and changed into an old pair of pants and a T-shirt.

I still had not shared my business plans with my parents or Kavita and Jay. But today was not a day to sit inside and talk. The sunshine and light breeze was calling me outdoors. I opened the side door. Something was different in my garden plot.

"Mom, come and see!" I called.

She followed me outside. One-third of my garden was full of finger-length Swiss chard leaves with colorful stems. The leaves were deep green; that shade of green also happens to be my favorite color. I was double happy.

"Doesn't my Swiss chard look great, Mom?"

"Yes. They're ready to be thinned out. If there are too many, they will be crowded," Mom said. "Without enough nutrition, they won't grow much. If you transplant the ones you remove, you can harvest more."

Trans-plant means to take a plant out from one place (or a pot) and put it in another place in soil.

I didn't want to do any more work on the crops I had already planted. Except harvest, eat, and sell them, of course. I didn't say that to Mom, because I didn't want to just throw away the extra plants.

"Should I transplant the Swiss chard into part of the pole bean space?" I asked.

"Yes, the beans will climb up so there will be enough space for the chard on the ground," Mom said.

"How come Jay doesn't need to thin his crop?" I asked .

Mom pointed to Jay's garden. "His spinach is not too crowded. He did weed his garden today though."

"When we were at the dance class?" I was kind of annoyed at Jay and sad for myself. Part of the fun was doing this with Kavita and Jay.

Mom patted my hand. "I know you wanted to garden with Jay. He told me that was the best time for him."

Then she showed me how to gently pull out some of the plants, roots and all. After Mom went inside, I dug new holes, a little away from the others, and replanted them.

Kavita brought out Megan's ukulele. Actually, now it was Kavita's ukulele, since Megan had given it to her.

Kavita plopped herself on the wood ledge and squirmed.

"What are you doing?" I asked.

"Making sure I don't fall off while I sing." She strummed the ukulele. A few seconds later she sang, *"Peas grow delicious and sweet. Peppers grow juicy and crisp. Potatoes become round and fat."*

Luckily, her singing was much louder than her strumming.

"It is so silly to play ukulele and sing to plants. They don't have ears," I said.

"I sang to the seeds," she said. "Look how much they have grown! Plants don't need ears to hear."

"You can't talk without a mouth and you can't hear without ears."

"Does the wind have a mouth?" Kavita asked.

"No."

She strummed her ukulele. "But it can howl and make a racket, right?"

"I guess."

"See, you don't need a mouth or ears to make noise or to hear."

She began singing.

"Why do—" I tried to say.

She gave me a stern look. "If we fight, the plants will be upset. Then they won't grow."

"But I think—"

I couldn't finish my sentence because Kavita put a finger to her lips and shushed me.

So while I thinned the Swiss chard, I listened to her songs and music. I hoped the plants were enjoying it more than I was.

Then I made an in-my-head list about Kavita's garden.

* Her pea plants do look good.

* Maybe I should ask her to sing to my Swiss chard plants.

* It might not help them, but it won't hurt them.

I raised my hand. "Yes?" Kavita asked.

"Could you sing to my rainbow Swiss chard?" I made sure to say "rainbow" because Kavita loves anything with the word rainbow.

"Sure." She sang, *"Rainbow chard, rainbow chard, oh so*

lovely rainbow chard! Beans, oh so beautiful beans, climb up fast, fast, fast."

"I haven't planted pole beans yet."

"Nina, doesn't Mom say it is important to prepare the soil before planting?"

"Yes."

"If you play music to the soil before you plant, you are preparing it. That way when you plant, the seeds will be going into happy soil and grow."

So, it's not just plants that like music—soil does too. Who knew?

Then Kavita sang for Jay's plants too, even though he wasn't there and some of his plants were not there either. *"Spinach, you're so green and good. Tomatoes red and juicy, I think you're so pretty. Pumpkins so cute and cuddly, grow round and oh so happy."*

By the time I was done thinning, I was also done listening to Kavita.

We both went in the house. Kavita put away her ukulele and I let out my breath.

Phew! No more music.

I wondered if the plants felt the same way. Were they whispering, "Yay! Finally, we can grow in peace"?

It occurred to me that maybe Jay didn't want Kavita playing ukulele and singing while he gardened.

Then I wondered when I should show my business plan to Jay and Kavita. We were growing vegetables together. I really needed to tell them about it soon.

But what if Jay and Kavita didn't agree? And I hadn't even asked Mom and Dad. Didn't I need to do that first?

Maybe I should wait a few more days and then decide what to do.

✳✳✳

It was May 20—the day to plant the pole beans. This time I had already soaked the seeds and now I took the bowl of seeds outside.

Kavita followed me. "Nina, look here."

I walked closer to her garden. "What is it?"

She pointed at the tiny green blanket of growth in her garden bed. "See those?"

"Are those weeds?"

"No way."

I tried to trick her. "Did you find them in Mom's seed collection?"

"No. They are my very own secret seeds."

If I asked Kavita what she had planted she wouldn't tell me—especially not if they were "secret seeds."

"Did you find those seeds in the mailbox?" I asked. Sometimes Mom gets a package of seed in the mail as a gift.

"Nope."

"You ordered them from a catalog?"

"Nope."

I threw up my hands. "I give up. Where did you get them? What are they?"

"You will just have to wait until they grow."

"OK."

The rainbow Swiss chard was growing well and so

were Kavita's peas and Jay's spinach. The spinach looked like it would be ready to harvest in a week or two.

I needed to concentrate on my own garden. Kavita watched as I dug a circle and dropped in the pole bean seeds. An earthworm crawled up from the hole.

"Our soil is so good. That means we will have great veggies," I said.

"Don't forget my playing ukually and singing to them." Kavita reminded me.

"Sure," I said. "Now can you help me find a trellis for the beans to climb on?"

"Like Mom has for the roses?"

"Yes."

"Maybe you can use a long stick."

"I don't think a stick will be enough. I need something sturdy."

"Long and sturdy,' Kavita said. "You can use the leftover wood we had from building the garden beds."

I spread my arms. "That's too wide."

Kavita put her hands on her hips. "You're too picky."

"Maybe I can use wooden stakes. Mom has a whole packet of them. Will you help me tie three of them together at the top?"

I went into the garage and Kavita headed inside the house. By the time I returned with the stakes, Kavita was waiting with a piece of string. I tied the string first to the three stakes. Then I stuck them into the dirt in the shape of a pyramid.

"Aren't you glad I got a long string?" Kavita asked.

"How did you know that we needed it?"

"I'm smart like that." She looked like she was hiding something.

"Mom told you, didn't she?" I asked.

"How did you know?"

"Because I am smart like you," I replied.

"Two smart sisters, planting gardens. Two smart sisters building a trellis," Kavita sang. I opened the door to head back inside.

"Two smart sisters walking in the house. Two smart sisters hungry for a snack," I sang.

CHAPTER SEVEN

"We're going to have a warm week," I told Kavita as we walked to school on Monday morning. "Maybe in a few days we will be able to harvest the rainbow Swiss chard."

After I had thinned the plants, my crop was growing really fast. Or maybe it was Kavita's music that made it grow fast, though I didn't want to admit that.

"My pea plants are blooming," she said. "How about we have Swiss chard with peas?"

I had never had those two vegetables together before and didn't know how that would taste. But whatever

Mom and Dad cooked always tasted good. "That would be delicious."

"What would be delicious?" Jay asked. He had snuck up on us.

"My peas and Nina's Swiss chard," Kavita replied.

"What about my spinach?"

"Wouldn't it be fun to have dinner together with all our veggies? Maybe your mom can make palak paneer," I said.

Palak is spinach, and paneer is an Indian cheese. In Wisconsin, we have a lot of cows, so we are called America's Dairyland. That means we have all kind of cheeses, including Indian cheese. Just thinking about creamy, tangy spinach and paneer made my mouth water. Even though it was morning and I never eat vegetables for breakfast. Except for potatoes. Plus, I'd already had breakfast.

"That way it would be bartering," Jay said.

"And it would be so much fun," I added.

"Now don't forget that my singing is helping your vegetables grow," Kavita said.

"We won't," Jay said. "You can have more spinach and Swiss chard than us."

By this time, we were almost at school.

"That's OK. I don't need more veggies." Kavita ran toward the playground, then stopped, turned around, and shouted, "You and Nina can have my share!"

It was nice of Kavita to offer us her veggies. I like them, but I don't want more than my share. And this was my chance to talk to Jay about my business plan.

"Jay," I said, "we don't need to eat extra veggies. We could sell them."

"Sell?"

"Yes, like they do at farmers' market."

"You need a license for that."

Was he joking? "We would need a license to sell extra peas and greens from our backyard?"

He looked serious as he hung up his jacket. "Sure do. I know because my great-uncle used to sell honey at the big market on the square. Also, a license costs money."

Tyler came toward us down the hallway. "Maybe we could just sell to neighbors," I said quickly. There was no reason to share this business idea with the entire school.

Jay shrugged.

I could tell that he didn't like my idea. It felt like I was missing the last few pages of a book I was reading. I didn't know what would happen to my business plan. It would have no ending.

That day, Ms. Lapin handed us our science quiz back. I glanced at Jay. He made a sign with his fingers. He had an A and so did I!

As we were getting ready to go home, Jay said, "I looked up whether plants can hear music."

I stuffed my books into my backpack. "Do they?"

"Certain kinds of music, like jazz, helps them grow. I am not sure if Kavita's ukulele or singing is good for our plants though."

"Let's keep that a secret from Kavita," I said. "She thinks all her ukulele playing and singing make them grow. If she found out it might help, she would play and sing more. If she found out it doesn't, she would be unhappy. If she found out it hurts, she would be devastated."

Dev-as-tat-ed means something happens that makes you sad. Then you fall apart.

Jay and I walked home with Kavita but managed to keep her from falling apart.

*** *** ***

But the next day I was the one who was devastated. When I was eating snack, I saw something.

Something furry. Something moving. Something munching.

In my garden.

A big, fat rabbit.

I ran out. The rabbit sprang from my garden to Jay's.

I chased it. It leaped off to Kavita's garden.

When I got there, it hopped back into my garden.

Round and round it went and I went right behind it.

I was huffing and puffing but not having any luck chasing away the rabbit.

Then I had an idea. I took a long stick. Now I could just stand in one place and wave the stick to get the rabbit out of our gardens. It worked! The rabbit jumped down from the raised bed and hid between a clump of ferns and lily of the valley under a birch tree.

I poked my stick into the growth, but it just stayed put. Maybe it had a burrow in our yard. Maybe it had family there.

I think rabbits are cute. But not so cute that I wanted them to feast on my vegetables. I had worked hard on my garden and wanted to have enough to harvest and even sell some.

When I came into the house, Mom was on the phone. I stood by the window, watched, and waited. I watched for the rabbit to come out of the clump and waited for Mom to be finished with her call.

"What are you looking at?" Kavita asked.

"At the rabbit that was eating my vegetables. It's hiding."

She crept close to the window, rested her nose on the glass, and peered out. "I don't see it hiding."

I rolled my eyes. "It's under the ferns and lilies."

"I want to see it," Kavita said. She put her shoes on.

Mom hung up the phone.

"A rabbit was chomping on my Swiss chard," I told her.

"Are you sure?" she asked. "How did it jump so high? Let's go check."

There were some Swiss chard stems and a few leaves left, but most of my plants were completely gone. Also, the bottom part of one of the pole bean plants was chewed up. I had been so busy chasing the rabbit, that I hadn't noticed how much it had eaten. Now my eyes stung.

"I'm so sorry." Mom put her arm around me. "I didn't think they could jump so high. Obviously, one has managed to do that."

"Nina, did you really see a rabbit?" Kavita asked.

"She did." Mom pointed at some small round brown things by the chewed-up plants. "And here is the proof."

Kavita and I examined the proof. Just with our eyes, not with our hands.

"Rabbit poop?" I asked.

Mom nodded.

"How come it didn't eat Kavita's peas and Jay's spinach?" I asked.

"I think it would have, Nina. You caught it just in time."

I brushed off my tears. "No, I was too late. It's not fair that it landed in my garden first."

"It's not. We should make sure it doesn't happen again." Mom walked toward the garage.

Kavita shook her head. "I don't want to put up a fence. I want a pet rabbit. If I play more ukually and sing, I'll have lots of peas. Then I can share them with my rabbit."

"I'm sure Mom and Dad won't let you have one for a pet," I said.

Kavita sang: *"A rabbit, a rabbit, wild and furry one. A pet to pat, the one I want."*

"The wild ones are not safe."

"A long time ago weren't they all wild?" she asked. "Like before the first people were born?"

Sometime I don't have answers for Kavita's questions. "I suppose."

"So maybe I can have one. I'll ask Mom. Where is she?"

"I think she is in the garage."

Kavita ran to her. I went inside the house and dialed.

"Hey," Jay answered.

"Hey! Can you come over and help put a fence around our gardens?" I asked.

"I don't need a fence."

I took a breath. "I guess not. If you want rabbits to eat your plants."

"Whaaat?" He shrieked so loud that I almost dropped the phone. I didn't think he was so attached to his vegetables!

"Then get over here."

"Be there in two minutes."

Jay was at our house in one. He also brought six tomato plants that he had started with seeds. They looked sturdy.

The great part of having a landscape architect Mom is that she has all the supplies for a garden. She gave us a decorative picket fence, only a foot tall and pretty.

"This fence will be easier to work with than a taller one," she said. "Even Kavita should be able to reach over it to plant and harvest. The fence should protect your plants from rabbit just fine," Mom said. "Unless it's a flying rabbit."

Jay and I pressed the stakes into the soil. Mom was right. It wasn't hard to put up. It made our raised beds look nice. And it would keep the rabbits out.

Jay began digging holes to transplant the tomato plants.

"Where is Kavita?" I asked.

"In the house," Mom said. "She found something in the garage to make a rabbit trap. Then she went in to get food."

"You know why she wants to trap rabbits, right?" I asked.

Jay set one of his tomato plants in a hole. "Because she wants to save her peas."

"Nope. She wants a pet rabbit," I said.

"A wild one?" he asked.

Mom sighed. "I should have known."

Kavita returned with a birdhouse made out of a gourd. She pointed to the hole. "See, I can put some carrots in there. Then I will leave it out in the garden. The rabbit will wiggle in. And then I'll have my pet rabbit."

"If it wiggles in, it can wiggle out," I said.

"No, it can't." Kavita handed Jay the birdhouse. "When you eat you gain weight, right?"

Jay peered into the hole. "If you eat too much and don't use the energy."

Kavita pulled out three carrots from her pockets and stuffed them through the hole. "Once a rabbit is inside and eats all these carrots, it will have too much food. It won't be able to run around, so it will get fat. It will be stuck inside."

Jay handed Kavita her contraption back.

Con-trap-tion means something you build or buy to help you do your work.

"Then how will you get your rabbit out?" I asked.

"I won't feed it for a day. Then it will be thin enough to slip out."

"Kavita, you're not going to keep a wild rabbit. They can carry diseases and be dangerous," Mom said.

"Is that the reason you don't want me to catch one?" Kavita asked.

"Yes," Mom said, as she headed inside.

"The pet store ones don't carry diseases?" Kavita asked.

"That's right," Mom answered over her shoulder.

"Then can we get one from a pet store?"

Jay and I were quiet as we waited for Mom's answer.

She stopped, looked back, and said, "NO. Wild or tame, we are not getting a rabbit."

For a moment, I almost thought Kavita had trapped Mom into getting us a pet rabbit.

CHAPTER EiGHT

Two whole days later, my chewed-up garden still looked chewed-up. It made me sad. It also took away my motivation for other things.

> **Mo-ti-va-tion** means when you feel something so strong that it makes you move. And you do it.

My garden was not growing and I was not moving. I read my business plan and felt even worse. If nothing grows there wouldn't be anything to eat. And there would be nothing to sell. I had worked so hard for nothing!

I made a different kind of list in Sakhi. Then I took Sakhi downstairs.

"Mom, you have a lot of patience," I told her.

Mom poured two glasses of milk for us. "Well, thank you."

I sighed.

Mom put the glasses on the table and sat down next to me. "What's the matter, Nina? What's bothering you?"

"The garden," I replied.

"Why?"

I showed her the list I had made.

Mom read. I reread what I had written over her shoulder.

Garden challenge list

* A garden needs many things: soil, sun, water, seeds, etc.

* Even after you get all that, you're not done.

✱ What a master of the garden needs is some luck.

✱ But it is difficult to find luck.

✱ They don't sell it in a store or even online.

✱ Even if someone has a lot of luck (like Kavita and Jay because the rabbit didn't eat their plants), they can't give it to you.

✱ I don't know much about luck.

✱ It's because I hardly ever have any.

I rested my head on Mom's shoulder.

She stroked my hair. "Sometimes things don't go as we plan. You can plant a garden, weed it, water it, and still don't get to harvest and enjoy your crop."

"But my garden had gone as I planned it. My crop of Swiss chard was growing just great until that rabbit ate it!" I said.

"Yes. But other things can go wrong, too. Plants can get

diseases; they can suffer if there is too much rain or too little rain. Plants can wilt if the weather turns too hot or too cold. All you can do is move forward."

"I can't move forward without my crop. Mom, how can I barter with Kavita and Jay if I don't have anything to give them?"

"Oh, my Ninai," Mom said and hugged me. She had not called me Ninai for ages. When Kavita was a baby she used to call me Ninai. Then Mom and Dad started calling me that sometimes.

"Ninai, don't be sad!" Kavita bounded into the room. "I'll share my peas with you. And Jay will share his spinach."

"Thanks. How do you know he will also share, when I don't have anything to trade?"

"Because he's your bestest friend."

It made me smile. I did have some luck.

It was because

✳   I have a kind sister

✳   A caring friend like Jay

* Mom who explains things so well

* On top of all that, I even have a stuffed Beaver named Lucky!

* In some ways they were all sharing their luck with me

***

That Sunday when Kavita and I were weeding, Jay came over with a wooden trellis. It was much nicer than the one I had made with three sticks.

"Is that for me?" I asked.

"This is for your mom's flowers," he said. "My dad and I made it."

I looked at my pole bean plants. "I guess I don't need one. My plants are already climbing up on the contraption Kavita and I made."

"Then you'd better not disturb them. But I will make three trellises in the winter. One for each of us to use next year."

"What a beautiful trellis," Mom said as soon as she saw it.

"Are you going to garden with us now?" I asked Jay.

"Your spinach has really grown because I have been playing music and singing to it, Jay," Kavita said.

Mom leaned the trellis against our house wall and came closer. "Jay, you need to harvest the spinach before it bolts."

"What does bolt mean?" Jay asked.

"It means it will run away," I said.

"Ha, ha!" Jay said.

"In a way Nina is right," Mom said. "When plants start seeding, it is called bolting. If you want to catch tender leaves, you have to pick them now."

"Can I harvest my peas?" Kavita asked.

"Sure," Mom said. She picked up the trellis and carried it to her flower garden.

Kavita ran in and got two brown paper bags. She handed one to Jay.

I felt sad. My Swiss chard was coming up again since

that fat rabbit ate it. But it wasn't ready to pick. "I have nothing to harvest. Can I help you?"

"You better, if you want to eat it," Jay said.

"If planting is fun, harvesting is twice as much fun," I said. "Thanks for letting me help you."

"Less work for Jay and me," Kavita said.

Jay gave her a thumbs-up sign.

✳✳✳

We harvested so much spinach that Meera Masi invited us for dinner. Then I was glad I hadn't said anything about selling it. She made spinach with paneer. She also made rice and Uncle Ryan picked up naan from an Indian restaurant. Naan is flat bread cooked in a clay oven. Dad made his famous curried garbanzo beans and potatoes. Mom had worked in the yard all day, so it was nice that she didn't have to cook.

Jay and I set up the tables while Kavita made place cards for everyone.

Mom cut a bouquet of pink and white peonies from our garden and brought them over.

We were just about to sit down to eat when Kavita asked. "What about my peas that we harvested? Can Nina, Jay, and I go home and get them?"

"Sugar snap peas are best raw. How about if you eat them for snack tomorrow?" Mom said.

'Tomorrow is the last day of school so let's celebrate with a sugar snap peas-party!" I said.

"Jay, will you come to our party tomorrow?" Kavita asked.

"Sure."

Kavita reached for my hand. "Nina, should we also invite Megan? She gave me the ukually and that is helping our plants grow."

"Could we, Mom?" I asked.

"Yes," Mom said.

Kavita was not only sharing her peas with me but also with my friends.

It made me happy.

CHAPTER NINE

The next day Megan walked home from school with Jay, Kavita, and me. We celebrated the start of summer break with a sugar snap peas-party. All four of us sat at the dining table.

"These are so sweet and crunchy." Megan picked up another peapod from the bowl.

"I sang and played the ukually to them," Kavita said.

"Why did you do that?" Megan asked.

"To make soil happy and make plants grow bigger," Kavita replied.

Megan glanced at me. Then she said, "That's why even their crunch is musical, Kavita."

Kavita beamed. "Do you want to see our garden?"

"Sure."

Kavita and Jay's garden looked so much better than mine. I didn't want Megan to see my rabbit-chewed vegetables. "Let's not…"

Before I could say more, Megan pushed back her chair. She grabbed the bowl. "Let's eat outside."

Kavita stood up. "I will get my ukually."

"Megan, get ready for a screechy treat," Jay whispered.

"Kavita, if you play your ukulele, how will you eat?" I said quickly.

"OK. I'll play it later. Let's go out."

Jay agreed. "An excellent idea."

Megan put the bowl on the picnic bench. I glanced at our gardens. Kavita's pea plants looked fine but not as beautiful as they looked before the harvest. Now that Jay had harvested spinach, his garden didn't look that great either. Actually, mine looked better than his.

I guess there are still differences if a rabbit harvests my vegetables or I do.

In-my-head list of the differences

* If a rabbit harvests, I get mad. If I harvest, I am happy.

* If a rabbit harvests, it eats by itself. If I harvest, I can share with family and friends.

* If a rabbit harvests, all my work is done for nothing. If I harvest, I get fresh vegetables as my reward.

Now that the fence was up, my Swiss chard was safe from rabbits. The days were getting longer, so the plants were growing fast. I would soon be picking my Swiss chard.

＊

On Saturday Mom, Kavita, and I woke up early to go to the farmers' market on the square. Mom doesn't like to go there when it gets crowded and I don't like it when they run out of my favorite pastry.

Madison is the capital of Wisconsin and the farmers' market is set up all around the Capitol building. The breeze from Lake Monona fluttered our hair as we walked up a block to the square.

There were lots of vegetable and flower plants, honey, eggs, some vegetables like radishes, asparagus, peas, and a variety of spinach and lettuce.

Mom got two bunches of asparagus. Kavita picked out sweet banana pepper and bell pepper plants. I stopped at a stand called Sugar Valley Farms.

There were so many different kinds of eggplants.

Their pictures were beautiful. I lifted up a tag. "Look, this Japanese eggplant fruit grows long and skinny."

"Nina, eggplant is a vegetable, not fruit," Kavita said.

"It is not," I said.

"We think of eggplant as vegetable but it's a fruit. You know why?" Mom said. "It's because it has seeds and grows from a flower."

"It's not as yummy as blueberries or peaches," Kavita said.

"It doesn't even taste sour like lemons. It's a funny fruit," I said.

I chose three different kinds of eggplants, two sturdy plants of each variety.

One was neon purple, the size of a mango. It was very pretty.

Another was white and looked like an egg. Just like its name.

The third one was the Japanese kind, long and slim.

"Do these look good, Mom?" I asked.

"Yes," she said. "Get them in your garden soon and they should grow well. Eggplant is very easy to grow. Did you know it is a native of India?"

"Then I will sing in Hindi when I play the ukually," Kavita told me. "That way your eggplants will grow faster."

"Then we will enjoy a bumper harvest," Mom said.

A bumper harvest!

Of eggplants?

I had no idea that eggplant was the easiest vegetable—I mean fruit—to grow. But really, when I eat eggplants, I don't think I am eating an apple, berries, or a banana. It is not sweet or even tart like lemon. To me, it is a vegetable.

Why did I buy three varieties of it? We might be eating eggplants every single day. I love stuffed eggplant and eggplant parmesan, but not every single day!

An eggplant a day was not a very happy thought.

I wished I had showed my business plan to my parents earlier.

"Mom, if we get a bumper crop, we should sell them. We could make tons of money," I said.

"I don't think you will have that many to sell," she said. "You only bought six plants."

"But what if we do?" I asked.

Mom paid for our purchases. "We can worry about that when the time comes."

I followed her around the curve. Mom was not thinking ahead.

"When we have a bunch of eggplants, then we will be sorry we can't sell them," I said.

"We can always give them away. I'm sure Meera Masi would like some," Mom said.

"Of course, Jay is part of our garden team so he can take as many as he wants for his mom," I said. "But what if we have tons more? Like coming out of our ears more? Can we sell them?"

"We'll see," Mom replied.

Mom didn't say "sure." But when I harvest baskets full of eggplants, she would really "see" them and would want to sell them. I felt much better about not having to eat all those future eggplants.

Mom bought us pastries stuffed with blueberries from a bakery stall.

As I ate the flaky crust and sweet, delicious berries inside, I closed my eyes.

I was lucky that they had not run out of my favorite pastry.

And this luck sure tasted yummy.

CHAPTER TEN

The next morning I woke up early. It was cloudy. I had learned a few things from helping Mom or just from listening to her. One was that it is best to transplant at a time when the hot sun won't wilt the plants, like late in the evening or on a cloudy day.

Today was cloudy, so it was the perfect day to transplant my eggplants from the pots to my garden. I wanted to sneak outside before Kavita was up. That way I could work without her playing the ukulele.

I carried the plants from the garage to my garden.

Mom was sitting on a picnic bench, enjoying her tea. "Do you need help?" she asked.

For a second, I thought it would be nice to have her help. But I also wanted to do it myself.

"Could you please watch me?" I said. "That way if I make a mistake you can tell me."

"Sure."

I made a list of steps in my head as I worked. That way I could write them down in Sakhi later.

My in-my-head list of how to transplant from a pot to a garden
✳ Dig holes that are a little larger than your pots.
✳ Gently loosen the plants from their containers.
✳ Then plop the plants down. One in each hole.
✳ Fill the soil around them.
✳ Pat and firm the soil.
✳ Water them well.

"You did a great job!" Mom said when I was done.

"Thanks." I took a few steps back and looked at them.

"Now what?"

"Now wait for them to grow."

"That's the hardest part of gardening," I said. "Why can't things grow fast, fast, fast?"

"Maybe when Kavita sings and plays the ukulele you can dance. It might help the plants grow faster." Mom was smiling.

"Don't tease me, Mom. I might just do that!"

The next day Mom helped Kavita transplant the pepper plants. I think she did most of the work while Kavita played the ukulele. I didn't dance though. I stayed inside and read.

***

School had been out for two weeks now. It had rained quite a lot in that time. That was good because I didn't have to water my garden. My pole beans had red blossoms and my eggplants had purple blossoms. And the Swiss chard plants had grown bigger.

So many rainy days were not good for me though. I was really bored today because Megan was at her uncle's farm and Jay was gone fishing up north with his cousins and Grandpa Joe.

I had nothing to do.

I took out Sakhi. My plan was there but I still had no name for my business.

I showed my plan to Kavita. "Do you want to help me come up with a name for our business?" I asked.

"Why do we have to name it?" she asked. "It's not our pet."

"Our business must have a name," I said. "Delicious Vegetables? Healthy Eats? Farm-fresh Foods?"

Kavita made a face. "I don't like any one of those."

"You're right. They don't sound unique or tempting," I said.

She nodded.

Kavita twirled. "How about Peas and Tease?

I said, "Or Yummy Beans?"

She smiled. "Swiss Chard in USA?"

"Instead of apple pie everyone can have Swiss chard pie for Fourth of July," I said.

We both rolled our eyes and began to laugh.

"I wish Jay was here," I said. "He could have suggested more funny names."

"He might not like the name we choose," Kavita said. "It's also his business, right? Should we wait?"

What if Jay hated our idea? Then Kavita might not want to do it. I would be a lonely business person. I didn't tell any of this to Kavita.

Instead I said, "If we come up with something special he would like it. Also, he could do a short dance show so we could have more customers."

"Yay!" Kavita clapped. "A free show."

"Yes. People will gather to see him. Then once they are there, they'll buy veggies."

She was quiet. Then she tugged at my arm. "When you sell vegetables can I play ukually? Please? That way we could sell more stuff."

"Actually, I'll need your help selling," I told her.

"But what about my ukually?"

How could I make her ukulele part of our business? An

idea wiggled by. We had bought the eggplants from Sugar Valley Farm.

I snapped my fingers. "We should call our business Ukulele Gardens."

Kavita eyes grew round. She nodded three times.

Our business had an exotic, island sound to it, so I was happy. And the word ukulele was in the title, so Kavita was happy. It was time for me to do more work.

On top of the business plan I wrote *Ukulele Gardens*.

"Kavita, we need to advertise by making up flyers to distribute to neighbors. We should write down location, time, and vegetables that are available," I said.

"Maybe we can ask Meera Masi to write her spinach-paneer recipe," she suggested.

"Great idea," I said. "By the time the next batch of vegetables come along, we could sell them."

This was so exciting.

CHAPTER ELEVEN

More rain! Mom said all the rain reminded her of monsoon in India.

Everything was soggy like a milk-soaked cookie. We didn't go out in the garden. It was a good thing that Kavita had a half-day cooking camp to attend, and I went to an art camp.

A rainy day here and there is fine, but after a few days, I missed the sun. I'm sure my plants did too. What if too much rain harmed them? Then there wouldn't be anything for us to harvest and to sell from Ukulele Gardens!

Then one morning I woke up not to the sounds of thunder or rain but to the warmth of sunshine on my face. I bolted from my bed and rushed to the window so quickly, I almost tripped on my blanket. The sun was shining and there were no dripping roofs or trees to be seen.

Jay came over after breakfast. I wondered if I should show him my business plan, especially since I wanted him to perform at the market. But he didn't have much time. It was better that we gardened rather than planned.

As soon as Jay, Kavita, and I started weeding, I spotted a big fat blob on one of my bean leaves.

A slug!

Ugh!

We checked our other plants. We didn't see any other slugs, but some of my bean leaves were chewed up. Unlike that rabbit, the slugs had damaged some of Kavita's and Jay's plants as well as mine. Where were they all hiding?

"We have to get rid of them. How do we do that when we don't even see them?" I asked.

Jay picked the bean leaf the slug was sitting on and dumped it into the weed pail.

Kavita clapped. "Now that slug will have lot of food to eat. It might invite other slugs to join him."

"Jay, can you please empty the weed pail in a garbage bag?" I asked.

"It's not even half full."

I didn't want to tell him and Kavita that slugs or most other bugs make me feel sick. "Please?"

I turned away while he emptied the weeds in a bag. That way I accidently didn't see the slug.

We must stop them from coming to our garden again, I thought.

Dad was puttering in the garage.

> Put-ter-ing is sort of like muttering. When you mutter you don't make anything clear.

When Dad putters in the garage he really doesn't make it any cleaner.

"Dad, what do we do so slugs never visit our garden again?" I asked.

He scratched his chin. "I don't know."

I turned to Jay. "My mom is at her yoga class. We'll have to wait to ask her."

"I have to go home soon."

I didn't want to deal with slugs after Jay went home. "Let's look it up," I suggested.

Jay and I looked online. There were many natural methods to get rid of slugs. We liked those because we didn't want to use any chemicals on our vegetables. Some of the ways, like trapping them, didn't sound good. Then we would have to still see them.

And drowning them in beer was even worse. Then I would have to deal with dead slugs! I just wanted them to never come again.

Finally, we found a good option. "Look! It says to sprinkle sand around the garden. That will stop them from visiting our plants," I said.

"But then our garden will turn into a beach," Kavita complained.

Jay and I both laughed.

Kavita stomped her foot. "It's not funny."

I hugged her. "Our garden won't turn into a beach. Don't worry—the plants will be fine."

Jay nodded. "A layer of sand will stop slugs from crawling into our garden. That's all."

"Why? Don't slugs like the beach?" Kavita asked.

"Nope," I said.

We went back to the garage. Dad was still there, puttering away.

"Do we have any sand?" I asked.

"Actually, I just saw a bag there," Dad pointed at shelves in the back. "What do you want to do with sand?"

"We want to make a slug-free beach," Kavita said.

"OK. It's pretty heavy. Let me carry the bag for you."

"Thanks, Dad." His puttering was helpful today. I didn't say that out loud though.

Jay, Kavita, and I covered all three raised beds with a layer of sand.

"What are those plants all over your garden?" Jay asked Kavita.

"Those are her mystery plants," I said.

Jay plucked a couple of leaves and sniffed. "Methi?" he asked.

"You're a great spy!" Kavita said. "Mom says they are called fenugreek in English."

We keep methi seeds in our spice box and Kavita must have taken some to plant.

I was impressed that Jay had figured out Kavita's mystery plant. I was also impressed that Kavita knew that methi was called fenugreek in English, and that she had thought to plant the seeds.

I had a smart friend and a smart sister!

Just think of what we three could do with Ukulele Gardens if the rabbits and the slugs would stay away!

When Mom came home from her class I told her, "We found a slug on my bean leaf this morning. Jay removed it. We also put sand around the plants so our vegetables can grow."

She looked happy-surprised. "That was the right thing to do!"

"I really like gardening, Mom."

"I can see that. And you are doing a great job solving problems like slugs and rabbits."

"With help from Kavita, Jay, and you."

"And now the weather is going to cooperate. We have had a wet spring and I was worried about plants getting water-clogged and roots rotting away." Mom pointed out the window. "Now there is no rain in the forecast for the entire week."

Yay!

Megan was coming over tomorrow. So double yay!

✳✳✳

I gave Lucky, my stuffed beaver, a good morning hug, brushed my teeth, and changed my clothes. When I went downstairs, Mom was humming. I also gave her a hug.

"Good morning, Mom! Are you happy because of the sunshine again?"

"I sure am. All the plants are growing so well."

"Let's look at my vegetables," I suggested.

Mom and I went to the window. My slug-free garden looked great from here. The Swiss chard leaves were long and ready to be picked. The beans looked like they had grown in just a few days of sunshine.

I gasped. There were so many red blooms on them!

Then we fell silent. A hummingbird fluttered over my bean blossoms. Its wings beat fast and furiously. It wasn't much bigger than a large butterfly, but it was a bird.

"Do you think I can go out to look more closely at the bird?" I asked.

Mom shook her head. "It might fly away."

"Then I'll stand here and watch."

"What are you doing?" Kavita asked from behind us. She was carrying her blanket and a stuffed rabbit.

"Watching a hummingbird."

She looked out. "Where is it?"

"It was on my bean plant. It just flew away."

"Come back amming bird, come back amming bird," Kavita called out.

"Humming, not amming," I said.

"Does it hum a song?" she asked.

"When it beats its wings, it makes a noise that sounds like humming," Mom explained.

"But it has no song to hum, right?" Kavita said.

"Right," I said.

"Then I will call it an amming bird. The hummingbird doesn't care if it is called humming or amming."

I shrugged. "OK."

The phone rang. Mom answered it right away. She listened first and then said, "Megan please take care. Here's Nina." She handed me the phone.

"Hi Megan."

"Nina, I sprained my wrist playing table tennis."

"Oh! Does it hurt a lot?" I asked.

"It does," she said. "There is a little swelling. My dad said I might have a hairline fracture. He wants to take me to our doctor."

I had been going to ask Megan if she still wanted to come over but I decided not to. She must be in pain. I could tell because she wasn't the usual Megan-on-the-phone person. She didn't talk nonstop and her voice was low.

"Take care," I said. "I'll miss you."

"Say hi to the plants," she said.

Megan was leaving for California soon, so I probably wasn't going to see her until almost the end of summer break. It was not fair.

I picked up a basket and a pair of clippers. "Since the bird is gone, I'm going out to harvest, Mom."

Kavita followed me.

She sang, *"Ammingbird, ammingbird, why don't you hum? Make up a song like me and hum, hum, hum."*

Even though I had just said to Kavita that it was OK for her to call a hummingbird an ammingbird, I felt irritated.

Ir-ri-tat-ed means something is not all smooth and comfortable.

Like an itchy sweater, my mind was all scratchy.

Maybe it was because of Megan's phone call and not Kavita's singing.

I tried to calm myself.

"Let's be quiet and see if the bird comes back," I said. I made sure I called it a bird. Which it was.

Kavita nodded. She was quiet for a few seconds.

"What does amming mean?" she asked.

I clipped Swiss chard and dropped the leaves carefully in the basket. The colorful stems looked so pretty. Just like rainbows.

"It doesn't mean anything," I said.

"Not in any language?"

"I don't think so."

"You can't be sure. Because you only know English and Hindi and there are hundreds of languages."

"Yes."

Kavita fluttered her arms like a bird. "So amming means a bird that tries to be a hummingbird."

I kept harvesting. "In what language?"

"In my new Kavitalish language. The one I am working on."

I rolled my eyes. "Who understands Kavitalish?"

125

"That bird does."

"OK." I should have stopped arguing with her a long time ago.

I went inside and took out some chard for Jay's family and some for our family. Then I looked in my basket. There was a little left, but it wasn't enough to open a farm stall.

"Mom, what should we do with the extra chard?" I asked.

She looked at the piles. "I think we'll need a lot more if you want to eat it more than once."

"Isn't this a lot? Or does it shrink like spinach and cabbage when we cook?"

Mom smiled. "It does."

I was disappointed that I didn't have enough to sell. But at least we had plenty to eat.

Maybe we will have lots of eggplants to eat, share, and sell.

CHAPTER TWELVE

By mid-July, my eggplants had two tiny fruits and tons of purple blossoms. Jay's tomatoes had small fruits, and Kavita's peppers had pretty white blossoms. Her potato-tops were leafy green. The scarlet bean flowers had produced many pods. Mom had already picked the methi leaves that Kavita had planted.

"Should I harvest the beans?" I asked Mom.

Mom moved closer to the window. "They are perfect now, young and tender. When they get bigger, they shouldn't be eaten raw."

"Why not?"

"They can be harmful."

I grabbed my basket and went outside. I snapped a bean. Even though it was young and tender I didn't eat it raw. There were more hanging on the plants. I had a basket ready to drop them in. But I couldn't do my job.

My in-my-head list of the bean harvesting problem

* They were pole beans. Which meant they grew high out of reach on a pole.

* On top of that I had planted them in a raised bed. That means that they were even higher than they would be if they were on the ground.

* I was still a child. That means I had not reached my full height.

My in-my-head list of my options

* Get a step stool from the house. (But it

was not that tall. It was just tall enough for Kavita to reach the sink to brush her teeth.)

* Wait for my height to catch up with my grown-up height. (Which meant I would have to wait years. That was not an option.)

* Find a grown-up person to help me.

* In my family, Mom and Dad were tall enough. But Dad was at work and Mom was busy. So that option was also out.

I wondered if the Crumps were home. I looked in their backyard; no one was there. I looked on the side of the house; no one was there. Then I walked up their driveway.

The big pile of dirt that they'd had there in the spring was gone. Plants were blooming in the round flower bed in the front yard. They looked beautiful—and I saw something else unexpected.

Could it be? I wondered. I tiptoed closer.

It was a nest with blue eggs in it. I watched as a robin fluttered in and out of it.

I was paying so much attention to the robin that when someone said, "Aren't those eggs lovely?" I jumped.

I turned to see Mr. Crump standing next to me. "Are you here for more soil, Nina?" he asked.

I shook my head. In the spring, I had taken some dirt from their pile to build a dam. It worked so well that I had almost flooded their basement. "No. I was wondering if you have a step stool I can borrow."

"I do. I was heading out to a coffee shop," he said. "Let me bring the stool out for you first."

Mr. Crump carried the stool to our yard. It was the perfect height.

"Thank you," I said.

Bean plucking is a two-handed job. You have to hold onto the vine with one hand and pluck the bean with the other. So, I kept my basket down on the ground and dropped beans into it.

For a while everything went well.

Then mosquitoes started buzzing and biting me. It was as if someone had sent them an invitation saying, "Come quickly for a delicious meal."

Both my hands were busy and I couldn't swat them.

Ugh!

One bit me on my ankle. I moved my foot.

Another bit my knee. I shifted.

That was a big mistake. I wobbled.

The next thing I knew I was on the ground, with the basket on my head. I must have knocked it over when I hit the ground.

The first rule of standing on a step stool is no jerking, no swatting, no shifting.

I just learned that after I fell off a step stool.

Mr. Crump ran over. "Are you OK?"

When did he get back?

"I am," I said. My feet were tangled in the fence and my head was resting on the ground. I had spilled beans on my face.

"Nina, I watched you fall. Are you hurt?" Kavita asked.

"No."

Before I could get up, I heard Jay. "Why are you on the ground?"

When had he come?

The worst thing about falling is not falling, or even getting a little hurt. It is the most horrible feeling when the whole WORLD sees you fall. Or asks why you are on the ground. As if you did that on purpose.

"I am fine," I announced to the whole world.

Mr. Crump extended his hand. I finally stood up with his help. I dusted off my clothes.

"Glad you're not hurt," Jay said.

I started picking up beans. "Yeah, me too."

None of them said anything more. At least they knew to be quiet.

Kavita went inside.

Mr. Crump left.

Jay helped me pick beans.

Then Kavita returned. With her ukulele, of course.

"Did you break a bone?" she asked.

I shook my head.

"Move around and let me check," she said.

"You are not my doctor."

She put her hands on her waist. "You listened to Montu and turned your tummy yellow with turmeric once. And he isn't your doctor."

Montu is our cousin who lives in India. I did listen to him once, and applied a paste of turmeric and salt to my tummy when I had a stomachache.

"If you play the ukulele, it might help Nina feel better," Jay suggested.

"That's why I brought it out."

I gave Jay a smile. He had distracted Kavita from being my doctor.

Kavita strummed and hummed. No words came out. Maybe she was making up a song.

Jay dropped a few more beans in my basket.

"Thanks," I said.

Another mosquito. I slapped my wrist.

Jay plucked a peapod from Kavita's plant and munched on it. "Mosquitoes love you," he announced.

I rolled my eyes. "Not just me. They like everyone. For their blood."

"Maybe. Though not equally."

"You mean they love me more?" I asked.

He nodded. Still munching.

"That's why I like to come outside with you, Nina," Kavita said. "When you are with me mosquitoes don't bite me. They like you more."

"That's it," Jay said. "Nina, the Mosquito Magnet."

"Thanks! That's the title I have been waiting for all my life."

"You deserve it," he said.

"What does that mean?" Kavita asked.

I explained. "To deserve means you have worked hard to have it."

"Why did you work so hard to get mosquitoes to bite you?" Kavita asked.

"You tell her, Jay," I said and turned to go inside. Let the mosquitoes bite those two.

"Oh. Aren't you going to pick more beans?" Kavita asked.

"I'm done."

"Then I better sing fast." *"Careful, careful when you pick beans. Bones, bones you don't want to creak."*

"Nina, stay," Jay said. "Listen to Kavita's song."

"So you don't get bit by mosquitoes?" I asked over my shoulder.

"Of course!" Jay said. "Wait, I have an idea to help you."

"You can tell me inside the house."

Kavita and Jay followed me in. They certainly didn't want to be out without the Mosquito Magnet.

Mom took the basket from my hand. "They look delicious."

"Thanks." I scratched my arm.

"Wash your hands and you can have cheese and methi parathas."

We washed our hands and sat at the counter. Mom served us parathas.

"Are these methi leaves from the seeds I planted?" Kavita asked.

"Yes," Mom said.

Kavita smiled. "Thank you ukually for growing methi!"

Jay and I ignored Kavita. As I pulled at a piece of slightly spicy, fluffy paratha, I asked, "What's your idea to help me, Jay?"

"There are plants that can keep mosquitoes away."

"You mean like citronella?" Mom asked. She sounded impressed.

"Yes. I couldn't think of the name, but that's it," he said.

I let the cheesy methi-paratha fill my mouth. It was soft and chewy. I just wanted to enjoy it without thinking about mosquitoes. I took another bite.

"Nina," Jay asked, "should we plant some citronella in our garden?"

"We don't have any room left. Maybe next year we can plant it," I said.

"We should think of a way to plant citronella this year," Jay said.

"Maybe you can come up with an idea." I shrugged. "Right now, I want to enjoy my food in the mosquito-free house."

CHAPTER THIRTEEN

I brushed my teeth and was ready to crawl in my bed, when I heard it.

Buzz...buzz...buzz...

A mosquito!

How did it get in my room? I tried to chase it out.

The problem with mosquitoes is sometimes they're too tiny to see. I couldn't tell if I had been successful. I couldn't see it, but that didn't mean it wasn't hiding somewhere, spying on me.

I had to find a mosquito solution. Not next year. Right now.

Lucky was sitting on my bed, patiently waiting for me. I picked him up, sat at my desk, and made a list in Sakhi.

How to fight mosquitoes

* Use a citronella plant. (But I don't have any room in my garden this year. My eggplants are taking up all the space.)

* Use bug spray. (But the smell makes me gag.)

* Find someone who is a more powerful mosquito magnet than I am. (I don't know anyone who is. And even if I did, I can't have them go with me every time I go outside.)

* Keep moving. I could keep dancing, so mosquitoes don't have chance to land on me. (That would be tiring. Also, how could I dance and garden at the same time?)

There was no good solution.

I got ready for bed and turned off my light.

Buzz…buzz…buzz…

I batted the air around my head with my hand.

The room was quiet for a few minutes.

Buzz…buzz…buzz…

I got up, turned the light on, and looked around.

Like a good hunter, the mosquito went into hiding.

I turned the lights off and pulled my blanket over my head. I kept a tiny gap right around my nose so I could breathe.

That was it! I had an idea.

I could drape something over myself. That way mosquitoes couldn't get to me.

Tomorrow I was going to make my own mosquito-proof device. I had to outsmart those buzzing pests.

✳✳✳

"Mom, do we have netting?" I asked the next morning.

"I think so," she said. "What do you want to do?"

"I have a plan."

Mom gave me the material. I waited until Kavita went to Avery's house to play. Then I spread it out flat and measured it. There was enough to cover me from head to toe.

I used my rain poncho as a pattern and cut the netting to the right size and shape. Now I had a netting poncho.

I was all set to harvest my beans, this time without the mosquitoes bothering me.

And then Jay showed up! Why did he always do that?

My in-my-head list of why Jay shows up unexpectedly
✳ Jay is my best friend, so he knows I want to see him.
✳ We are also family friends. (His mom and my mom visit each other without calling. I guess he thinks he can too.)
✳ He is my neighbor. It is easy for him to visit. (He doesn't have to walk far.)

When he saw my new poncho, he asked, "What's that?"

"It's my Mosquito Proof Device." I slipped it on. "MPD."

Jay laughed.

"Jay Davenport, it's not funny," I said.

"Maybe not to you," he said. "Look in the mirror."

I looked ridiculous.

> **Ri-dic-u-lous** means you had better get rid of whatever you are doing, wearing, or thinking. Because it makes you silly.

"Your turn," I said as I slipped it off.

Jay put it on.

I pointed to the mirror. "Come see."

"I look even more ridiculous than you did," he said.

"I agree."

He danced. I danced. We both danced our mosquito dance. Then we laughed until tears prickled our eyes, and then we went outside.

Jay handed me a spray bottle. "Here, now you won't have to do the mosquito dance outside."

It was a bug spray made with citronella oil. It smelled good.

With the help of my friend I was armed against the enemy. We picked a lot of beans, and got no mosquito bites.

"That's good amount of beans," Mom said when she saw what Jay and I had harvested.

There were enough beans to eat and sell. Before I could tell Mom about my business plan, she filled two bags. "It is so nice to share such fresh produce," Mom said. "Jay, please take one bag home. Nina, please give the second one to Mr. and Mrs. Crump."

I had to share with Jay and with our neighbor. After all, I had borrowed Mr. Crump's step stool to harvest.

When Kavita came home from Avery's house she saw the leftover beans in the basket. She rushed out and came back with her ukulele.

"Should we share some beans with Megan's family?" she asked.

"They are in California," I said. I hadn't seen Megan in a long time and I missed her.

"Then can I share the beans with Avery's family, Nina?" Kavita asked.

"Sure," I replied.

I guess Kavita had completely forgotten about Ukulele Gardens. It was okay. Jay and I had had a lot of mosquito-madness fun that day. I was also happy sharing beans with everyone.

It bothered me to keep my business idea a secret from Jay for all this time though. It was as if our friendship had a wrinkle in it.

But maybe I didn't need to worry. We might not have enough of anything to sell.

CHAPTER FOURTEEN

One day in early August, Jay and I helped Kavita harvest a few potatoes. They were red and the size of a fist.

"My potatoes are so…so…amazing," Kavita said.

Jay nodded. "I bet they're also delicious."

I had a great idea. "What if Mom makes pakoras for snack?"

"Yes!" Kavita and Jay both said at the same time.

We picked a few eggplants. "Maybe she can make eggplant pakoras for herself, Dad, and your parents," I said. "We have a lot of them." Mom, Dad, Meera Masi, and

Uncle Ryan love eggplant pakoras. Kavita, Jay, and I, not so much.

Out of nowhere, Kavita said, "We have a business called Ukulele Gardens to sell extra veggies."

I gasped.

"A business? To sell? Our stuff?" He stared at me. "When were you going to tell me?"

"I...I was going to. I tried to...and then, you know, it didn't happen."

"It didn't happen because you didn't make it happen. How could you have a plan and not tell me?" He pointed to our raised beds. "These belong to all three of us. Not just you and Kavita."

Jay's green eyes were so full of anger that they seem to change color. I didn't know what to say.

I made a quick in-my-head list.

* I had kept Ukulele Garden a secret. That made Jay furious.

* But I had told Kavita about it. I bet that made him double furious.

* I had messed this up.

* What was I going to do?

Kavita pulled at Jay's arm. "If you dance we could sell even more eggplants at Ukulele Gardens."

He folded his arms. "I can't believe you even assigned me a task, but forgot to tell me anything about it. How nice!"

"Are you being sar...sarcas...something, Jay?" Kavita asked.

"Sarcastic, Kavita." I turned to Jay. "I'm so sorry. I haven't even talked to my parents about it, so I don't know if we're allowed to sell. Plus we don't really have enough to sell. It was just a fun idea that Kavita and I talked about."

"That's not the point," he said.

"Well, I tried to tell you about selling once," I told him.

"When?"

"At school. I thought you were not interested."

He looked confused. "Are you sure?"

"First I suggested the farmers' market. You said we needed a license. Then I said maybe we could sell to neighbors. You just shrugged. I thought you didn't care for my idea."

"I remember you talking about the farmers' market, but nothing about selling to neighbors," he said.

I threw up my hands. "Maybe you should pay more attention when I tell you something."

"I always do. You just have too many ideas in your head. Maybe you think you told me, but you never did."

"I did tell you!"

Kavita put up her hand. "If you two fight, our plants will be sad. They won't grow."

Tears pricked my eyes as I brushed them off with the back of my hand.

Jay turned away. Was he leaving? Kavita looked as miserable as I felt.

Jay marched a few steps. Then he stopped. "Oh no! Nina, your bean plants are full of holes."

"What?" I rushed over. "What is happening to them now?"

Kavita came close. "See those bugs?" she said. "The ones that are pretty like ladybugs but are not ladybugs?"

I looked closely. Kavita was right. There were bugs on my plants. They were shimmery and shaped like ladybugs, but they weren't red with black dots.

"You think these bugs are chewing up my bean leaves?" I asked Kavita.

Kavita sang, *"The bugs on the leaves go chomp, chomp, chomp. The bugs on the leaves go chomp, chomp, chomp, all through the plant."*

Sometime Kavita's singing makes sense.

"Are you really sure, Kavita?" Jay asked. "You think those bugs are making the holes?"

He was still here!

"As sure as I am about my singing," Kavita said.

I had to ask Mom what to do.

The potato-filled basket was heavy and I couldn't lift it. Jay gave me a hand. Without my asking.

"Thanks." I said.

He didn't say a word as we walked inside the house.

Mom was in the kitchen. "What's wrong?" she asked.

"My bean leaves are full of holes."

"I think it is because of those shiny, brownish bugs," Kavita said.

"I'm sorry, Nina," Mom said. "It sounds like some Japanese beetles have found your plants."

"What can I do to get rid of them, Mom?" I asked.

She handed me a paper cup. "Fill this with warm soapy water. Pull the bugs off one by one and drop them in it."

"Ewww, I don't want to do that," I said. "Isn't there something we can spray?"

"Removing them by hand is the best way. It is also the safest and most effective. We don't want to spray chemicals on the food we are going to eat."

I did want to get rid of them safely. I would have to pull them off.

I took the hot soapy water outside. Jay and Kavita followed me.

"Jay, do you want to get rid of these Japanese beetles?" I asked.

"Why? They're on your bean plants," he said. "You need to do it."

"You know how I can't stand bugs."

"Then ignore them. Just like you ignored me."

"I'm sorry. I didn't mean to hurt your feelings," I said.

"It's OK," he mumbled.

I tried to hand him the cup. "Jay, please take care of the Japanese beetles before they get on your spinach and tomatoes too."

He didn't take the cup. "I am not doing it by myself. We both have to get rid of them."

He got another cup of soapy water. I handed him a pair of garden gloves. I also wore some.

Then we went bug hunting. Kavita watched us as we dropped the Japanese beetles in the cup.

"If they're Japanese beetles, why are they in the United States?" she asked.

"Good question," Jay said. "I don't know the answer. Do you, Nina?"

"I think people come to this country from all over the world," I said. "I guess the bugs must also come here from all over the world."

"You are right," Kavita said.

After we finished hunting the beetles, we went to the kitchen.

"Mom, could we have pakoras for snack?" I asked.

"Sure," Mom picked up a few potatoes from the basket. These will make great pakoras."

Soon, the scent of pakoras filled me with happiness. We washed our hands and sat at the counter.

We don't make fried food often, so this was a special treat. My mouth watered when I saw potatoes sliced, dipped in batter, and fried to a crisp golden color.

"These are hot, so you need to wait to eat them," Mom said, as if she knew I was going to stuff one in my mouth. "Get plates and something to drink. I will serve you some in a minute."

Jay brought out the dishes, I filled three glasses with water, and Kavita got three napkins.

I didn't tell Mom about our Japanese beetle hunt.

Who wants to talk about bugs when you are eating? It would ruin our appetite.

Ap-pe-tite means you're hungry and ready to eat.

So I stayed quiet and once the pakoras had cooled, I enjoyed my food.

The problem with pakoras is you can keep on eating and eating them. After we finished the first serving Mom gave each of us a few more. "That's it for today," she said.

"But I am still hungry," Kavita whined.

I pointed at the pakoras Mom had just served us. "You won't be after you finish those."

"I will be. I know my stomach better than you do."

"Kavita," Mom said. "If you are hungry after this you can have some fruit."

After Kavita finished the second serving, she said that her stomach was no longer hungry. But maybe she was like me. I still wanted more because they tasted so good. But I knew Mom would not give us more. All three of us took our dishes to the sink.

"I'm sorry I didn't talk to you about the business earlier," I whispered to Jay. "Come to my room and I'll show you the plan."

We went up to my room. I opened Sakhi and handed it to Jay. Kavita and I quietly waited until he finished reading. He closed the notebook.

"I like the name of the business. I like the plan." He held up his hand. "But I will not dance."

"That's OK."

"I can always sing," Kavita said.

Oh, no! That would drive customers away, I thought. I glanced at Jay. He seemed to be thinking the same thing.

"Since I didn't get a chance to help make the plan I should get to decide something," Jay said.

Kavita nodded.

"We don't need singing, dancing, or playing," Jay declared.

"Then how will we sell all the vegetables?" Kavita asked.

"Actually, we don't have many to sell," I said. Another idea came to my mind. "We could share the rest with neighbors or even give it to a food pantry."

"That's a great idea," Jay said.

"Do you think I can play ukually and sing at a food pantry?" Kavita asked.

"I guess you'll have to ask for their permission," I said.

Jay and I smiled at each other.

Phew!

Before Jay left, Mom gave him a plateful of pakoras to take to his family.

"Thank you," Jay said.

"Now make sure you don't eat any before you get home," I said as he left.

"We'll see," he whispered. His eyes twinkled. "I'm really glad you asked your mom to make these."

"I think he's going to eat some of them," Kavita said.

I closed the door. "For sure."

"Not fair," Kavita said.

"Tell that to Mom."

"No, you tell her."

"Nope."

We both knew not to complain after Mom had made such a special snack.

Mom gave me a platterful of pakoras to take to the Crumps.

Kavita and I took it right over, because pakoras taste best when they are warm.

Mrs. Crump opened the door. "Come in, come in."

Kavita and I followed her into the kitchen.

"Ahh! It smells delicious," she said as soon as I handed her the plate.

"They're pakoras," Kavita said.

Mrs. Crump's forehead scrunched in confusion.

I lifted the aluminum foil. She looked at the plate as if they were not golden pakoras but gold coins. "These are our favorites," she said. "Thank you so much!"

"It is so nice that Mom also makes pakoras for our neighbors," Kavita said as we walked back. "Mr. and Mrs. Crump love them."

"Everyone likes pakoras," I said.

"You're right. Maybe we should open a pakora shop. I will grow the potatoes. You can peel them."

"Who will slice and fry them?"

"Dad and Mom."

"You mean a family pakora shop? That's not a bad idea," I said. "We could have a food cart. We are going to have so many eggplants. We could also make some pakoras out of those. Maybe we should call them gold coins in case people don't know what pakoras are."

"Yay!" Kavita's eyes reminded me of Mrs. Crump's eyes when she saw the golden pakoras.

Round and sparkly!

I like all the ideas that come rolling down the various tracks in my head. The pakora-selling plan had excited Kavita and me but what about Mom and Dad?

"We need Mom and Dad's permission about the pakora-selling," I told Kavita.

I also wondered if we needed a license for a food cart. And how much it would cost.

After dinner that night, Kavita and I talked to Mom and Dad.

"Kavita, Jay, and I were planning to sell the vegetables we grow to our neighbors, but we decided to share instead," I said.

"Or give them to a food pantry," Kavita added.

"That's a good idea," Dad said.

Mom pointed at Sakhi. "I suppose you have made plans for this?"

"No, but we did make one for selling before we decided to share." I opened Sakhi and showed them our business plan.

"Ukulele Gardens! What a lovely name," Mom said.

"The plan is quite good," Dad said.

"Could we donate extra vegetables we harvest this year?" I asked.

"Of course," Mom said. "But remember the growing season will end when frost comes at the end of October."

"But we already have so many eggplants," I said.

"Don't forget my peppers," Kavita added.

Another idea came to my mind. "We can also plant peas, Swiss chard, and spinach for fall."

"You both must also get ready for your school year. Once school starts you won't have much time to garden," Dad said.

I looked at Kavita. She looked like she was about to cry. I felt the same way.

"This year was your first year to garden and you have learned a lot. Maybe next year you can apply all the things you have learned and be really good gardeners. You can even make your garden bigger. Then you'll have a lot to share," Mom said.

"Maybe we can have a food cart and sell pakoras?" Kavita asked.

Mom and Dad looked at me and smiled. I wondered why.

"Yes, maybe then you can become an entrepreneur," Dad said.

En-tre-pre-neur means someone who starts a business.

CHAPTER FiFTEEN

School was about to start. Kavita's peppers were growing well. My eggplants plants, all six of them, were full of fruits. Jay's tomatoes were turning red.

We shared the eggplants, tomatoes, and peppers with our neighbors. Still, there were more veggies left, so we took some to the food pantry. Jay's tomatoes and Kavita's potatoes and peppers were the biggest hit with everyone. I mean who gets tired of eating tomatoes, potatoes, and peppers?

The pumpkins were getting bigger and rounder and the Swiss chard, spinach, and peas were growing again.

Mom said as soon as the weather turned cold, the plants would slow down.

My beans still had red flowers. We would keep getting beans for a while yet. And unlike the eggplants, I was not tired of them.

Then I noticed something wasn't right.

The flowers weren't turning into tiny beans. The tiny beans weren't turning into big beans. Was someone eating them?

"You have to be a better spy," Kavita said when I told her what was happening.

I inspected my bean plants again.

To **in-spect** means to check very carefully.

Then I made a list of what I needed to do.

I opened Sakhi and wrote.

How to save the beans

* Stay by the plants, day and night. (Not

possible because I need to eat, sleep, shower and, pretty soon, go to school.)

* Put up a burglar alarm for plants. (I don't think there is one, which means I would have to invent it first.)

* Cover up the plants. (But then they wouldn't get any sunlight. Without sunlight they wouldn't grow.)

Then I thought about the hummingbird coming to the bean flowers to drink nectar. Could a hummingbird be eating the beans? But if so, why hadn't it eaten them before?

I went outside. A blue jay flew away from my garden.

That's it. The blue jay or other birds or maybe squirrels must be eating my bean blossoms. How could I scare them away?

"I will hang a picture of an eagle in the garden. That way, blue jays and other birds will stay out," I told Kavita.

"That's a good idea. I can draw you one," Kavita offered.

"Thanks," I said. "The paper eagle will get wet in rain. We'll have to use something else. Aluminum foil and color with permanent markers?"

"Let's start," Kavita said.

She covered the dining table with newspapers so the markers wouldn't stain it. I took out a roll of foil and tore off two large pieces. I gave one to Kavita and kept the other for myself.

We began our work.

"What are you two doing?" Mom asked.

"We are making eagles to keep the birds away from my beans," I said.

She came closer. "Those eagles look scary."

"Do you think other birds will be scared?" I asked.

"Only one way to find out."

Then I had another idea. "Wait, what about making a scarecrow to really scare them off? Could we do that, Mom?"

"Sure," she said.

Kavita was so excited about this new idea, she jumped around and left her half-drawn eagle on the table. "Can I dress the scarecrow?"

"First we have to build a scarecrow. Then we can worry about dressing it."

What could we make a scarecrow out of? Usually, when I start a new project I like to make a list in Sakhi. Today, I didn't have much time though.

"Let's go to the garage and figure out how to make a scarecrow," I said to Kavita.

We looked at all the things that were in the garage.

* Two cars
* Dad's old bicycle
* A tricycle
* Two kids' bikes
* Rolls of chicken wire
* The birdhouse made of a gourd that Kavita had not used to catch a rabbit

* Two snow shovels

* A broom and a dustpan

* Two wheelbarrows

* Mom's gardening supplies and tools like trowels, flowerpots, stakes, and gloves (They covered an entire shelf.)

* A plastic kiddie pool (That was the one we had soaked the newspapers in.)

"Let's use the birdhouse, shovels, and brooms to build a scarecrow with," I said.

"That birdhouse is for rabbit catching," Kavita said. She was not happy.

"OK, let's use something else," I said.

But I could not come up with anything else.

"I'm going inside," Kavita said.

I followed her inside.

Then I had an idea. "Wait in the kitchen, Kavita. I'll be right back."

I ran to my room, grabbed something, and came downstairs.

"What's that?" she asked.

I opened up the net poncho I had made for myself. "It's called Mosquito Proof Device, but it will work for birds and squirrels too," I said.

I didn't want to climb up the step stool and try to put the net over the stakes and fall. I asked Mom for help.

She laughed when she saw what I wanted to do. "Very creative," she said. "Your poncho won't scare the birds away but it will keep them away from the bean plants."

We covered the bean plants with the net poncho. It was perfect!

"How about the pumpkins?" Kavita asked.

"They don't need it. The birds are not eating them."

"But the pumpkins might feel bad if they don't get to wear a poncho," she said.

"How about if we give them a new layer of compost?"

She asked, "Hi pumpkins, would you like that?"

Luckily, a breeze stirred the leaves on the pumpkin vines. "Kavita, they're nodding."

Kavita and I top-dressed the pumpkin patch with mulch.

To **top-dress** means to scatter on top.

Now the pumpkins were happy and so was I.

We also hung half-drawn eagles for extra protection.

✳✳✳

A few weeks later the beans were getting big under their netting, the pumpkins were the size of tennis balls, and we were back in school.

After school one day, I wrote about my garden in Sakhi. It was a list and thoughts all mixed together. It was a rambling thing. Just like plants.

Garden Notes

Jay, Kavita, and I had started a vegetable garden. I thought it would be easy for me to become a master of the garden.

These are the reasons I thought that

* Mom is a gardener and I was getting help from her.

* I knew a garden needed soil, seeds, water, and sun.

* So I thought I only had to provide soil and seeds.

* Nature would provide sun and water.

* Everything would grow beautifully.

* And all I had to do was harvest, eat, and sell.

It didn't work that way. The gardening was much harder than I had imagined.

Somehow, I couldn't just drop the seeds in and watch the garden grow. The first day we had to soak the newspapers and line the lawn, help nail the garden beds together, and haul the soil and compost to fill the beds.

Phew! It was tiring.

And we hadn't even started planting!

Then I thought all I had to do was

* Plant

* Weed

* Harvest

* Maybe cook (Some vegetables, like eggplants, have to be cooked.)

* Eat!

In my mind my garden was supposed to be filled with vegetables. It was supposed to be a visiting place for colorful butterflies, hummingbirds, and bees, and a home for earthworms.

But I didn't realize other things that could play a part.

* Too much rain

* Too little rain

* Weather that was too hot

* Weather that was too cold

* Slugs and other bugs and birds

* And the worst of all, rabbits!

* For the gardener, maybe the worst was all the mosquitoes.

Mom was right about learning through gardening. It was almost like school. While growing a garden, I have learned so much about plants and also about people.

Lessons from gardening

* Gardens are unpredictable. Sometimes friendships are too.

* Sometimes plants hurry up and grow quickly, sometimes they are lazy and grow slowly. Just like people.

* Sometimes plants get attacked by rabbits and slugs, just like people get sick from germs and bugs.

* Plants like sunshine, water, and food, but just in the right amount. Just like people.

* Do plants like music and singing? I am not sure. But it doesn't seem to hurt them People also like music but maybe not the screechy type.

I was not a master of the garden the way I thought I would be by now. In the garden, I was not in charge. My Swiss chard got chewed up by a rabbit. The pole beans were attacked by slugs and Japanese beetles, and then eaten by birds.

My eggplants did amazingly well. So did Jay's tomatoes and Kavita's peppers. Maybe the plants that did well all liked the same growing conditions. The ones Mother Nature created this year.

So I guess Mother Nature was in charge. She always is.

She controls rain, sun, wind, and temperature.

She also controls other things too. Like all the critters, bugs, and birds.

Even a master gardener like Mom had to wait for Mother Nature to cooperate.

I was lucky to have helped build three raised beds, and to plant, weed, fight bugs, and to have harvested and eaten vegetables that I grew. I was lucky to do all this with Kavita and Jay. I was lucky to share our harvest with family, friends, neighbors, and the people who come to the food pantry.

It was nice to see a smile on Mrs. Crump's face when we delivered pakoras. We were all happy when Jay and Meera Masi shared spinach and paneer with us. Kavita was excited when Megan gave her the ukulele.

Maybe that is why Mother Nature doesn't sell things, she just shares.

Maybe next year we could build a garden for kids who don't have one. We could start one at school. I would have to talk to Jay and Kavita about it though. This was not just my project. It was our project and they were my partners. I had to share my thoughts with them and hear their ideas before making any plans.

I was so excited about all this. I mean next year we would be ready with all the things we have learned about gardening. We could be very successful.

If Mother Nature cooperated.

> To **co-op-er-ate** means to work together like a team.

I looked out at our backyard. Some leaves were already changing colors. Soon the growing season would come to an end. I would always remember my first garden. It was the year I had become a Mosquito Magnet, a netting-poncho designer, a garden spy, and a bug and slug hunter—but not a master of the garden or a business owner.

That was OK.

As long as I have new ideas that keep roaring down the tracks in my brain, I have all the luck I need.

MEET THE AUTHOR!

Kashmira Sheth was born in India and came to the United States when she was seventeen to attend Iowa State University, where she received a BS in microbiology. She is the author of several picture books, chapter books, and middle grade and young adult novels. In her free time, Kashmira enjoys gardening, traveling, and spending time with her family. She also enjoys making lists—but not as much as Nina does! Kashmira lives in Virginia.

www.kashmirasheth.com

Q: Who or what inspired the character of Nina Soni?

A: My daughter Rupa inspired the character of Nina Soni. She is curious, intelligent, helpful, and enjoys doing projects, as does Nina. My other daughter, Neha, inspired Kavita.

Q: Like Nina Soni, you are also Indian-American. Do any of Nina's experiences remind you of your own childhood?

A: There were a few of my childhood experiences that I was able to weave in to Nina's story, like rubbing oil in my hair. Nina and I also share a love of Indian cuisine. In that way there is similarity between my childhood and hers.

There are differences too. Since I grew up in India—in a different time and culture—some of my childhood experiences are not directly relatable to Nina. I used to travel to my elementary school by a horse-drawn buggy and Nina has never ridden in that kind of horse buggy!

I have tried to capture some childhood experiences that are universal, regardless of time and place. For example, Nina wants to be helpful, she worries about Jay and their friendship, and she misses her father when he is away.

Q: Why do you think it's important for readers to be exposed to diverse books written by people who share those identities?

A: Imagine looking in a mirror and always seeing other people's images. That is how it is for many readers who come from minority backgrounds. When these children read books, or watch movies or TV shows, they never see themselves in the story. The message they get is that their journeys are not important or worthy of being told.

When a writer with a particular identity writes a story that includes characters with that identity, the writer knows nuances of the experiences of that group. This richness of knowledge seeps into the story, making it layered and believable for all the readers, and particularly the ones who share that identity. Those readers can see themselves reflected in the story—not as a shallow, stereotypical caricature, but as full, truthful, and meaningful characters.

Q: Many of your stories focus on family. What does family mean to you?

A: Family has always been a cornerstone of my life. I grew up not only with my parents but also with my grandparents, my great grandfather and extended family members. As an adult, I lived not only with my husband and children, but also (at various times in our lives) with extended family members. My mother still lives with me. I love to spend time with my grandchildren now. They keep me connected to my readers, inspire me, and challenge me.

Q: Because your mother tongue is Gujarati, have you faced any challenges writing books in English? What do you find is the biggest difference between Gujarati and English?

A: My mother tongue is Gujarati but Nina's family speaks Hindi at home. Nina's story is written in English. So I get to juggle all three languages.

Each language has its own strength and beauty. It is sometimes difficult for me to find the right word or a phrase in English that I have in my mind in Gujarati or Hindi. At other times there is no cultural equivalent for certain rituals or ceremonies and I end up having to describe them. The same thing happens with food. For example, if someone says I had toast with orange marmalade, most readers would know what the texture and taste of it would be like. If I write I had khakhra (sort of toasted roti) with murabba (raw, sour mango marmalade) I have to explain that. Done too often, it can get tiresome and take a lot out of the story. Done sparingly, it can add depth and richness to the story.

English is rich in verbs whereas Gujarati and Hindi are rich in nouns. It is such a luxury to use different verbs in English to make the action come alive. But describing a physical thing in English becomes harder for me. For example, when I write in English, I keep using the same word for sun or moon, but in Gujarati and Hindi I have several choices.

Q: How have your past jobs inspired your writing?

A: I studied microbiology and worked in that field for many years. It wasn't until I started reading with my two daughters that I thought about writing. My science background seeps into my writing. In *Nina Soni, Former Best Friend,* you can see her mentioning mold and doing a pH experiment with red cabbage juice. I taught dance for several years and Nina takes Indian dance classes similar to the ones I taught.